More raves for Ira Berkowitz's *Old Flame*

"Taut, convincing and flat-out terrific."
—*Fredericksburg Freelance-Star*

"Violent and entertaining. . . . Deftly rendering such New York City neighborhoods as Alphabet City and Brighton Beach (Little Odessa), Berkowitz keeps the dialogue rough, the action fast, and the characterization thin but sharp as Jake steers his way through the myriad traps thrown in his way." —*Publishers Weekly*

"Just the tonic to cure the blues. . . . Pour yourself a healthy shot of bourbon, drink it in as few gulps as possible and settle back with a reminder of how hard-boiled fiction used to be done, updated to reflect what is being done right now." —Sarah Weinman, *Baltimore Sun*

"A tightly written, deftly plotted gem of crime fiction . . . Steeg and a half dozen other characters are memorable creations, and the dialogue is clever and gritty. Best, though, is the portrait of Hell's Kitchen and its denizens, who predate gentrification." —Thomas Gaughan, *Booklist (starred)*

"Grade: A. There will always be a surfeit of authors using Hell's Kitchen as a backdrop for their private-eye tales, but Berkowitz is in the lead—and it will take a doozy of a tale to catch him." —*Rocky Mountain News*

"Cynical, wisecracking, and full of snappy dialogue, *Old Flame* is a valentine to hard-boiled fiction fans. If Berkowitz doesn't write more books about Steeg, I may send a goon to sock him in the kisser."

—Chelsea Cain, *New York Times* bestselling
author of *Heartsick*

"A mean, lean piece of noir full of tough talk, hard men, and harder women. It's a tense walk down a dark alley, a heart-pounding chase on the gritty streets of New York that ends with a punch in the jaw. Ira Berkowitz flicks his cigarette ash at the noir greats and dares them to do it better."

—Lisa Unger, *New York Times* bestselling author of
Beautiful Lies

"A sharp, clean, and precise piece of crime writing, *Old Flame* is not to be missed. Ira Berkowitz drops you into Hell's Kitchen and leaves you wanting for more."

—Michael Harvey, author of *The Chicago Way* and
cocreator of *Cold Case Files*

"A good old-fashioned crime novel crowded with fast-talking, colorful characters, each of whom comes with a secret or two and the temperament of a killer. It's hard to put down."

—Thomas Perry, Edgar Award–winning author of
Silence, The Butcher's Boy, and *Nightlife*

"In Hell's Kitchen, *Old Flame* burns white-hot. If gritty New York streets and rough-and-tumble detectives turn you on, read this book."

—Reed Farrel Coleman, Shamus and Anthony
Award–winning author of *Soul Patch* and
The James Deans

SINNERS' BALL

IRA BERKOWITZ

SINNERS' BALL

A JACKSON STEEG NOVEL

 THREE RIVERS PRESS NEW YORK

Copyright © 2009 by Ira Berkowitz

Published in the United States by Three Rivers Press, an imprint of the Crown Publishing Group, a division of Random House, Inc., New York.
www.crownpublishing.com

Three Rivers Press and the Tugboat design are registered trademarks of Random House, Inc.

Library of Congress Cataloging-in-Publication Data
Berkowitz, Ira.
    Sinners' ball : a Jackson Steeg novel / Ira Berkowitz.—1st ed.
        p. cm.
    1. Ex-police officers—New York (State)—New York—Fiction.   2. Family
secrets—Fiction.   3. New York (N.Y.)—Fiction.   I. Title.
    PS3602.E7573S56 2009
    813'.6—dc22   2009 015453

ISBN 978-0-307-40863-1

Printed in the United States of America

Design by Chris Welch

10 9 8 7 6 5 4 3 2 1

First Edition

FOR PHYLLIS

SINNERS' BALL

PROLOGUE

Angela was a tiny fifteen-year-old runaway with flyaway hair, a face filled with hollows dense with shadows, and minutes left to live.

She had been in the city just shy of two months. Her older sister, Wanda, had run a year earlier, leaving Angela alone in their father's house.

You gotta get out, Wanda had said. *I know what it's like. Know what he's like. Ma won't admit it. Probably glad he don't mess with her. It ain't gonna stop, Angie. Quit being a fraidy cat. Come to New York and live with me. It's cool. The people. The scene. All cool. There's work. I'll hook you up. Pays more money than you ever seen.*

But Angela had been a fraidy cat and stayed, kidding herself into believing it would stop.

Until the last time.

While he slept, Angela had crept into the garage, lifted all the cash from his secret hiding place, and headed for the Greyhound bus station in Davenport. Twenty-two stops and a little more than a day later she pulled into the Port Authority bus depot. Wanda met her and took her back to an apartment she shared with three other girls and a man they called Daddy. He told Angela she was part of the family now, and in his family everyone worked. Then he told her what work meant.

Angela ran. Again.

Until the streets caught her.

Now it was Christmas Eve. The temperature had dipped into the low teens and the wind blew the snow sideways. The sidewalk Santas were long gone, the carolers had packed it in, and all across the city, families, all warm and cozy, tossed the last piece of tinsel on the tree and settled in for the night.

And in Hell's Kitchen, Angela and two brain-fried junkies she had met outside a warehouse hatched their own plan to celebrate the Savior's birth.

The guys—one with rat eyes, and the other with sores on his face—had dug deep into their pockets and come up with enough for a dime bag of rock and the best bottle of wine three dollars could buy. Even though the thought of it made her feel as if spiders were crawling all over her skin, Angela chipped in her body for a couple of hits and a few hours of warmth.

Then they jimmied a window and climbed into the warehouse.

Christmas Eve was for families, and it had been a long time since Angela had seen her sister. Rat Eyes handed her a cell phone he had boosted a few days earlier. Wanda didn't answer, but Angela left the address.

And then it was party time.

Surrounded by stacks of cartons stuffed with counterfeit designer goods, they'd made short work of the rock and polished off the bottle with lying stories of Christmas Eves past. Now, with eyes closed and heads propped against the cartons, they slept.

They never heard the whisper of flame smoldering deep within the walls or the frantic rustling of rats scurrying to the safety of the river. Never smelled the acrid odor of smoke as the flames crept up toward the dead space just under the roof.

Wanda sat in a musty West Side bar nursing a two-buck draft in a dirty pint glass, listening to Angela's message and weighing her options. Outside, the streets were empty, shrouded in the muted glow of light filtered through giant flakes of whipping snow. She wasn't even close to making her three-hundred-dollar nut, and didn't have a prayer. Not on a night like this. But there was one thing she knew for a certainty: Daddy didn't want to hear shit about blizzards, or Christmas, or any other stuff. You live in Daddy's house, you pay the rent. Every day. No ifs, ands, or buts.

Wanda reached into her brassiere and pulled out a thin wad of bills. She added them up one more time, thinking maybe she had made a mistake. Nope. Three twenties and a ten.

Fuck it! she thought, staring down at the thin soup at the bottom of the glass. *If I'm gonna get a beating, it's gonna be for a good reason.* Besides, the warehouse wasn't too far away.

The flames were streaming through the windows on the lower floors when Wanda came up the street. Splashes of glass glittered like diamonds in the snow. She stood stock-still, her body unwilling to move. A man, standing across the street with his face framed in firelight, turned to look at her. The expression on his face made her guts shrivel. And she looked away.

When she looked back, he was gone.

Hearing the distant whine of sirens, Wanda glanced back at the building and swiped a sleeve across her eyes.

1

need you to meet me at Feeney's. Noon tomorrow. It's important.

My brother, Dave, had finally decided to drop into my life.

It had been a Job-like year for my brother. He had always been pretty good at dodging bad fortune, but in a few short months he had hit the cosmic trifecta. An Israeli mobster's bomb blew off his left hand. His son, Anthony, blew off Dartmouth for a spot in the family business. Soon after, his wife, Franny, blew up their marriage. And Dave never saw any of it coming. In a heartbeat his confidence went down the tubes, and he turned into a recluse.

It had been a long time since I'd heard from him. Then the message on my answering machine.

It got my attention. Words like *need* had never been part of Dave's vocabulary.

The next morning I awoke to the sight of frost on the inside of my windows. During the night the boiler in my apartment house had finally gone belly-up, and my three rooms were as comfy as a meat locker. Outside, clouds the color of sewage hung ominously over the city. Snow was definitely on the way.

When I arrived at Feeney's, a Closed sign hung on the front door. The usual deal when my brother wanted complete privacy.

A young, wiry-looking guy with shoulder-length blond hair stood next to the sign, smoking a cigarette and eyeing me with a piranha grin. As I reached for the doorknob, he sidled up real close.

"Can't you read, rummy?" he said. "The sign says you're gonna have to find another slop chute to drink your breakfast."

The snakes in my head awakened from their slumber and began to uncoil. It had been a while since they had graced me with their presence. Truth be told, I'd missed them. Especially at times like this.

"Who the hell are you?" I said.

With a toying grin, he put the flat of his hand on my chest.

"The guy who tells you where you can or can't go."

Maybe it was the stupid grin, or the hand on my chest, or that the boiler in my apartment building had committed suicide. Nah, it was the "rummy" crack.

My left hand shot out and grabbed his hair, tugging

his head toward me. The move kind of shortened the distance between my right hand and a spot just above the bridge of his nose. He went over as if he had been hit with a cattle prod.

I reached down and dragged him into Feeney's, leaving his unconscious body just inside the door.

Nick D'Amico, the proprietor and one of Dave's deceptively jolly killers, was deep in conversation at the bar with Kenny Apple, another of Dave's hit men. But my dramatic entrance got their attention.

I walked over to the bar and jerked my thumb at the body.

"Who's the new guy?" I said.

Nick sighed. "What the hell happened?"

"Your doorman has an attitude problem."

"*Fuck!*" Nick said. "He ain't one of mine. Name's Tommy Cisco. He's with Anthony's crew."

"Anthony has a *crew*?"

"He thinks he does. What can I tell you?" He walked over, grabbed a handful of Cisco's coat, and dragged him back outside. "Be right back. Gotta take the garbage out."

"Nice work," Kenny said.

Kenny Apple brought new meaning to the word *schizoid*. An orthodox Jewish accountant by training who traded in his ledger books for a gun. How he managed to square that with his faith was a continuing mystery.

"He pissed me off."

"What a surprise."

"What's so important that I had to come out on a day like this?"

"You got anything better to do?"

"Actually, no."

Ever since the NYPD and I parted company, my plate has been pretty much half-empty. Sometimes more. There's not much call for an ex–Homicide detective with one lung and a disability pension. Every now and then something comes along, and if it interests me, I handle it. The pay is usually crap, but I don't need much. The rest of the time I spend trying to figure out what to do with the rest of my life. At least, that's what I tell people. The truth is I did figure it out, and didn't like the answer.

"How about a heads-up about what I'm walking into here?" I said.

"Dave'll tell you."

"He has *another* problem?"

"You might say. You better get over there, his blood's really up."

Nick had done a nice job putting Feeney's back together after the bomb that took Dave's hand had gutted the joint. The mahogany bar, the Wurlitzer, the tin ceiling with a fleur-de-lis hammered into every panel—everything looked as good as new.

The same couldn't be said for my brother.

Feeney's was where Dave did business, and as usual, he was dressed for it. Navy blue pin-striped suit. Crisp, white shirt. Soft gray tie. But that's where the resemblance to the *old* Dave ended. His eyes were listless recesses set in a face that had lost its certainty. The stump of his left hand was encased in a sheath of black leather, which he rubbed furiously against the pebbled remainder of a port-wine stain on his cheek. It was an endlessly humiliating blotch of congenital graffiti that even laser surgery couldn't completely erase.

When Dave rubbed his cheek, bad things were in the offing.

After the Israeli's bomb had nearly taken my brother out, he had become a lot more cautious. He and Anthony sat at a back booth that afforded him a panoramic view of everything that went on at the saloon.

After the bombing, in some truly convoluted act of loyalty, Anthony had decided he wanted in. Another thing Dave never saw coming. In a truly screwed-up act of parenting, Dave agreed.

It won't last, he said. *The kid's too soft for the life. Doesn't have the stomach for it. He'll be back in Hanover carving ice sculptures at the Winter Festival in under a month.*

That made my brother oh for four in the prediction department.

Now Anthony, the avid apprentice, sat by the master's side soaking up the ins and outs of organized crime. He flashed me a cold smile he had probably spent weeks rehearsing in front of a mirror.

Dave threw me a bemused look.

"Cisco couldn't make it in on his own?" he said.

"You forgot to leave my name on the guest list."

He smiled and shook his head. "And people say *I'm* on a hair trigger."

"So, how're you doing?"

"Living the dream." His voice was a scrape of sandpaper, so low I had to lean in to hear it.

Anthony giggled as if it were the funniest thing he'd ever heard.

Anthony was the family hope, and I loved him like a son. A gentle boy with brains and a heart who was a sure bet to make us proud. And he threw it all away. The sight of him working hard on becoming his father's Mini-Me was enough to make me sick. I shot him a look and the stupid giggle froze in his throat.

Our little byplay didn't escape Dave's notice.

"What're you so pissy about, Jake?" he said, using the nickname he'd tagged me with when we were kids.

"If you don't know, I'm sorry for you."

My brother waved his hand dismissively. "Don't worry about it," he said. He looked at his watch. "You're late."

"Really? Last time I checked, I'm not on your payroll."

"That may be about to change."

That got my attention.

"What's that supposed to mean?"

"How's Allie?"

"Fine. As soon as I finish here, I'm meeting her and DeeDee for lunch."

Allie Lebow and DeeDee Santos were the two women in my life. Allie was my current and future love. DeeDee was my best buddy and kind of a surrogate daughter. She and her father lived in my building. Unfortunately for DeeDee, he was a frequent guest of the city's penal institutions. And her mother had split to the Dominican Republic. That left DeeDee pretty much on her own, and headed for a life on the streets. No way would I let that happen. Now she was a sophomore at one of the most prestigious high schools in the city.

"Allie's a keeper. And DeeDee, too," he said, smiling now. "That kid has some mouth on her. Always liked her."

"She'll be thrilled to hear it. Now, can we get back to that *payroll* thing again?"

"Remember that fire I had over at my warehouse?"

His tone was dismissive, as if it were a kitchen flare-up that took out a couple of oven mitts, rather than a three-alarmer that turned three squatters into stains on the floor and took the lives of two New York City firefighters.

"Sure. Christmas Eve."

"The DA is saying it was arson, and that I did it for the insurance money."

"You don't need the money."

"Right."

"And his evidence?"

"Far as I know, zip. But our esteemed DA always plays things close to the vest."

"That he does," I said.

"The warehouse was insured by Pytho. Their guy who investigated the fire was supposed to be here by now."

"But he's not."

"He called. Running late. I want you to hear what he has to say."

"I'll drop by after lunch."

"That works. Look, you know how this is going to go down. The DA is all about expedience. He looks at my line of work, puts two and two together, and comes up with the brilliant deduction that I torched the place. I take the fall for felony murder, another case cleared. Crime wave over."

Sad to say, my brother's analysis was dead right. This was an election year, and politics trumped everything. The DA had been in office since there were trolley cars. But he wasn't quite ready for a retirement home. There was one last hurrah on his to-do list. A high-profile case starring my brother, the reigning Hell's Kitchen's Kingpin of Crime, would fit the bill very nicely.

"You pretty much summed it up," I said.

"My lawyer tells me that an indictment is about to come down."

"Based on what? Someone who could place you at the scene?"

"Not possible. I wasn't there."

"And you have an alibi."

"Are you kidding? Airtight."

"Then its gotta be coming from the competition. What's the word on the street?"

"Nada. The doers could be the Guineas, the spics, the Russians, or some other flavor of asshole thinking about trying me on for size. Since the uh, incident"—he stroked his cheek with the stump of his hand—"the jokers probably think I'm, you know, vulnerable. But they don't know who they're fucking with, do they?"

They surely didn't.

He smiled a crooked smile. "When I find them, I'm going to rip out their eyes."

Nothing ever changes.

"Have you heard from Franny?"

His face went cold.

"She's yesterday, so screw her. From here on in it's just the two of us. Just like old times."

Just like old times!

Something in my brother's face sparked an unsettling thought.

"You've told me everything?" I said.

He smiled. "See you after lunch."

2

"Why do I do this to myself?" Allie said.

Café Buffo was a watering hole for folks in the ad business. Every year, on the third Friday in January, the restaurant honored the industry's movers and shakers. Their caricatures went up on the walls, and their names were attached to menu items. Allie had yet to make the cut. This year was no different. The winner was busy taking his bows when I arrived.

"No luck, huh?" I said, easing into a seat opposite her and DeeDee, who suddenly looked older to me. Maybe it was the lighting. Or maybe it was something new.

DeeDee had always been kind of a tomboy, wearing whatever was handy. But today she wore freshly pressed jeans and a black tank top, and her long black hair was lustrous and neatly combed. Most disturbing, her eyes sported just a hint of mascara. Allie noticed my confusion and greeted it with a raised eyebrow and a *things are changing and you better get used to it* smile.

Even in the depths of depression, Allie, the love of my life, looked terrific. Her honey-colored hair was pulled back in a ponytail. And under a furry vest she wore a T-shirt that announced WHAT MAKES YOU THINK I GIVE A DAMN?

"Ignored again," Allie said. "The winner, an unctuous little brain with a Brit agency, walked off with top honors for a campaign for fly-front adult diapers."

"Fills a need, I guess," DeeDee said. "Who wants to see grown men with wet blotches all over the front of their pants?"

"I think you're missing the point, kiddo," I said.

"Out of the mouths of babes," Allie said. "It's target marketing at its best. Zipper. Button. And Velcro. An incontinent's dream." She shook her head. "To top it all off, he's maybe thirteen, and doesn't even shave."

"Why do you put yourself through this?" I said.

She looked over at the winner posing with his carica-ture as cameras flashed.

"Look at him. Besides being totally bereft of talent, there's no sign he's hit puberty yet! I lost to a brainless fly-front-adult-diaper schlockmeister child."

"Why do you care what these imbeciles think?" DeeDee said. "Besides, he looks retarded."

She did have a mouth on her.

"Good question. Maybe, it's a Rift Valley–size masochistic streak. Or maybe, it's a yearning for the occasional pat on the back for writing ads that make the cash register ring. Do you know what it's like to write copy and then have it turned into a rag by clients, account schmucks, researchers, lawyers, and other assorted *experts* who turn to Hallmark for help in saying happy birthday?"

She plucked a pencil-thin breadstick from the breadbasket and inserted the tip between her teeth. For Allie this was lunch.

"It must suck," DeeDee said.

"You think? Imagine wildebeest at a lion buffet." Allie threw up her hands. "What's the use?" She shook her head and tried for a smile. "How's your day going, Steeg? Battling the forces of evil and keeping the world safe from itself?"

This wasn't going to be pretty. My brother wasn't exactly on Allie's fave list.

"In a manner of speaking. Dave has a . . . situation, and needs my help."

Carefully placing the breadstick with the barely nibbled tip on her plate, she took the news without expression. "You're going to work for your brother," she said.

After a too-long pause punctuated by a really deep sigh, she continued. "Why?"

"Hate the sin, love the sinner," I said, using one of the many stock lines I had developed over the years to deflect that specific question.

"That's too pat by half, Steeg. Look, because he's your brother I tolerate him. But he has this little problem that I find a tad vexing."

"And that is?"

"His vocation is killing people."

"No one's perfect," DeeDee said, rising to my brother's defense. "Besides, he's always been nice to me."

I could have kissed her! For DeeDee it was all about family—and Dave was family.

"Wonderful! Look, it'd be bad enough if he just killed his own kind. But the bomb that was meant for Dave nearly cost Steeg his life." She turned to me. "So I ask again, why?"

Not a bad point. I was outside of Feeney's when the explosion ripped it apart.

"Two reasons."

I told her about the fire.

"I have a really serious problem when justice is asymmetrical."

"What does that mean?"

"When the DA decides to pin someone to his personal butterfly collection board—especially an easy target like my brother—things like guilt or innocence go out the window."

"Maybe the DA is balancing the scales for the other crimes your brother's gotten away with."

"Not supposed to work that way. Besides, if it were Dave's handiwork, there wouldn't be any bodies to find."

"Good point, Steeg," DeeDee said.

"Dear God!" Allie said, shaking her head.

"You wanted honesty."

"And the other reason?"

"You're an only child, right?"

"Where's this going?

"Call it the pull of blood. I'm all he has."

"You've got to give him that," DeeDee said.

"I would if this were a debate, DeeDee, but it's not. It's that little thing we call life." She turned back to me. "That's very noble, Steeg."

"Not really. Sometimes the law is an axe poised over the wrong bare neck."

"And that's where you come in."

"Pretty much."

Allie thought about that for a few moments, trying hard, I guess, to understand what life with me really meant.

"All right," she said. "For now. But there's one thing you have to promise."

With Allie, you were never quite home free.

"Name it."

She reached over and ran a fingertip across my cheek.

"Be careful," she said.

Once again, all was well with the world.

"I can't believe that warehouse burned down," DeeDee said.

"Things happen," I said.

"I was there right after it was closed. Nick took Justin and me there a few months ago. Said he was getting rid of stuff and told us we could have anything we wanted." She fingered the hem of her tank top. "Where do you think I got this?"

A tiny little paternal alarm bell went off.

"Who's Justin?"

DeeDee's cheeks reddened just a bit.

"Justin Hapner," she said, in a way that made his name glow like neon. "He goes to Devereaux Academy with me. He's a senior."

Devereaux was the city's premier private school and had had the good judgment to give DeeDee a full scholarship.

"Where does he live?"

"Brooklyn. Bensonhurst."

With that address, I figured Justin for a scholarship kid too.

"How come you never mentioned him?"

"Enough with the questions."

"I like to know about your friends."

She glanced out the window, and jumped up from the table.

"I've gotta run."

"Where're you going?" I said. "You haven't even eaten."

"Justin's outside," she said, pointing to a gangly kid in a hoodie pacing out in the street. "We're going to a concert at the South Street Seaport."

She was out the door in a flash.

I turned to Allie.

"What was that all about? I figured we'd spend the day together."

She smiled. "It appears your little girl has grown up."

3

On my way back to Feeney's, Benny Kim flagged me down.

Benny was the latest incarnation of the folks who made Hell's Kitchen vibrate like a Charlie Parker saxophone riff. People of dark melodies whose harmonics were all fluid and harsh. Men who'd left the old country behind and bowed to no one.

Now the Irish and Germans who'd built the railroad, worked the docks, run the rackets, and operated rotgut bars and whorehouses on every corner were pretty much gone.

Except for throwbacks like my brother.

The new kids on the block were Koreans like Benny, and Guineans, Jamaicans, Indians, Somalis, and a sprinkle of yuppies to leaven the mix. All trying to make it. And their music was as dark and rough-edged as that of the hardscrabble people they'd replaced.

But Benny Kim was one of a kind.

In a city full of wannabes, he was a true artist. And his greengrocery was his canvas. Fruits and vegetables and flowers in all their glorious hues were nothing more than paints on his palette. A daub of kiwis here, a tumble of Yukon golds there, a splash of blood oranges fronting rolling mounds of Granny Smiths.

A vibrating work of karmic balance.

But Benny was also a realist, and he never let art get in the way of commerce. Most of his time was spent stripping week-old roses of their outer petals and peddling them as new.

I noticed that a fresh helping of scaffolding decorated the building adjoining his. Attached to the woodwork was a sign that read FRANCO DEMOLITION. The real estate barons were interring another dead soldier in Hell's Kitchen's graveyard, and were well on their way to turning the city into a Hollywood set. A friend of mine, guy named Danny Reno, grew up in that building. He came to a bad end too. The thought didn't put me in a cheery frame of mind.

"What's up, Benny?" I said.

"You cops ain't worth a shit!"

"And a top o' the morning to you, my man. Some L.L. Beaner drop a kiwi in the radish bin again?"

He put down a fading bunch of white roses with cerise centers and pink edging on their petals. "My new Beemer, Steeg. Gone. You know how much endive I gotta sell to buy a Beemer?"

"A bushel and a bunch of pecks, I suspect."

"You make jokes and my insurance rates are circling Mars. Patel? Runs the electronics store? Him too. Check-cashing guy down the street? Him too. The dry cleaner? They stole his Escalade. What do you think of that?"

"Nice cars. I'm definitely in the wrong business. What do the friendly folks at the neighborhood precinct say?"

"*Too bad, Benny. Doing everything we can, Benny. Maybe we find your car, maybe not. Call your insurance company*." He thumped his chest. "Fucking cocksuckers!"

"Why're you telling me this?"

"Who else am I going to tell? No one else wants to listen anymore. From now on, I'm gonna be the eyes and ears of this fucking neighborhood."

"Maybe you should think about parking in a garage."

"Where do you think the bastards took it from?"

I was out of suggestions.

4

The Closed sign was still up at Feeney's.

Nick met me at the door.

"DeeDee said you took her and her friend to Dave's warehouse," I said.

He seemed annoyed by my question.

"Is there a problem?"

I was annoyed by his answer.

"It's counterfeit. Ergo, illegal. And I don't want her around it."

"The stuff was gonna wind up in the garbage anyway."

"She needs something, I'll buy it. Understood?"

"You live in a sewer, you're gonna get dirty. Can't protect her forever, Steeg."

"Sure I can. Now tell me about her friend."

"Nothing to tell."

"Did you talk to him?"

"Are you kidding? When my kids hit their teens, I stopped talking to *them*."

"They must have appreciated it," I said.

He jutted his chin toward the back. "Dave's waiting."

My brother and Anthony sat across from a heavyset, cherubic guy. He appeared to be doing all the talking, punctuating each sentence with a twitch of his brush mustache.

I walked up to them.

Dave nodded at the cherub. "Jake, this is Sal Lomascio. We go way back."

We shook hands.

Sal pulled his briefcase off the seat and set it on the table. I squeezed in next to him.

"Let's take it from the top," I said. "Tell me why it was arson and not some bonehead with a cigarette, or a short in the wiring?"

Anthony looked at me as if I were the dumbest guy in the room. "It's not that simple," he said.

Dave beat me to it.

"Shut the fuck up, Anthony," he said.

My nephew's eyes wobbled for an instant. Then they fixed on his father with a tightness I had never seen before. Anthony had gone from being the favored son to being a minion. And he wasn't handling it well.

Welcome to your new life, kid, I thought.

"It was arson," Sal said. "No doubt about it."

"And you know that, how?"

"It's my job. Dave tells me you were a cop, so you know it ain't like in the movies. You know, where the handsome lead detective spots this mook standing on the fringe of the crowd with his eyes rolling around in his head like he's about to come. Then he grabs the freak and hammers him until he confesses."

"I love movies like that. Always made me feel good about my career choice."

"But in my world it's all about forensics."

"So you found an accelerant."

His mustache twitched. "No. But lots of circumstantial stuff pointing that way. Goes a long way to convincing a jury. And it starts with the real estate market."

"Hell of a circumstance."

"You bet your ass it is. Ever since the subprime mortgage bubble blew all to shit, real estate prices dropped off the cliff. Properties like Dave's that were on the market at gonzo inflated values suddenly slid twenty, thirty percent or more, and went begging even at the discount. So, what's an owner to do?"

"If you can't make a flood, make a fire," I said.

"Exactly. And Pytho has had a bunch of them lately. Sloppy, amateurish jobs."

"Tough to find good help these days."

"Tell me about it," Sal agreed.

"But that wasn't what happened here."

"Nope. Whoever did this was no amateur. Two points of origin." Sal's eyes twinkled, and his mustache gave a self-congratulatory twitch. "That was the first clue. It took a lot of looking, and the answer was in the char-ring."

"And that revealed?"

"The doer bored holes in the lath-and-plaster walls, stuffed them with newspapers, and lit it up."

"Burns low and slow," I said.

"Right. You had a classic fire tetrahedron—fuel, oxy-gen, heat, and what eventually became—as we say in the arson game—an 'uninhibited chemical reaction.'"

"I don't get it. Lath is metal, and plaster doesn't burn."

"That's now. Unfortunately for the stiffs, the ware-house was built around 1900. Back then the lath was wood."

"Not a happy circumstance."

"I know. Like you said, everything was going on real slow inside the walls. But when the Red Devil hit the wooden flooring and made it to the crates full of all that Chinese import shit, it just had more to eat. Took a couple of hundred firefighters with their snot turned to icicles to put it out. It was one hairy job."

"Show me the photos," I said.

"Thought you'd never ask."

He dipped into his briefcase, came out with a file, and passed it to me.

I opened it and pulled out four close-ups of the walls.

"Kind of hard to read," Sal said.

Actually, they weren't. Each photo showed a spot on the wall where the charring was more pronounced.

"What about the sprinklers?" I said.

"Piping was fucked. I figure before the party got started, the celebrants tried to rip out the pipes, sell them, and maybe do some Christmas shopping. With brass going for close to two bucks a pound, they could score enough shit to last a few days. But all the poor bastards managed to do was break the pipe that fed the sprinkler."

"You said there was a party. Why?"

"An empty bottle of wine near one of the bodies. Ain't exactly a leap of logic."

"Fascinating, but total circumstantial bullshit." I looked over at my brother. "What's going on here?"

He turned to Sal.

"Tell him," he said.

"We found six bodies in the basement," Sal said. "In packing crates."

"I told you there was more," my brother said.

"That little fact somehow missed the newspapers," I said.

"The DA never released it to the press," Sal said.

"Let me get this straight," I said. "There were two crime scenes. Both primary. One with the squatters on the main floor. And the other with six bodies in the basement?"

"Fucked up, huh? But just when you think it can't get better, it does."

"I can hardly wait."

He reached into his briefcase and pulled out three photos. "These are the shots of the people who bought it on the main floor."

Three bodies. Two men and a woman. Curled up in a fetal ball.

Only two possibilities.

A defensive posture they assumed when the flames reached them. Or they were already dead, and dehydration had contracted their muscles.

"Has the medical examiner ruled whether they were alive when the fire took them?"

"ME's report hasn't come in yet."

I made a mental note to call my ex-partner Luce Guidry to see if she could get her hands on it.

Sal then passed me the photos of the guys in the basement. All I could make out were six packing crates that appeared to be totally burned.

"Not much to see," I said.

"I know," Sal said. "Gotta wait on the autopsy."

"I don't get it," I said.

"Neither do I," Dave said. "I put the warehouse on the market six months ago, locked it up, and walked away. No one had access."

"What about the counterfeit stuff?"

"Ever since the latest fed crackdown, I got out of the business. Left it to the Chinatown gangs. Too much risk, not enough reward. Whatever Nick couldn't move on the street, I left sitting there, growing mold."

"And you have no idea where the bodies came from?"

"Not a clue."

"Any IDs?

"Let's put it this way," Sal said. "They were so fucked up they're gonna be down to checking dental records."

"Can I have your files?"

He handed me the folders. "Knock yourself out. They're copies."

"And you'll let me know if you hear anything else?"

Sal snapped the briefcase shut. "Absolutely."

"So what do you think, Jake?" Dave said.

"First blush? Two sets of vics. Two separate crimes."

"Way I see it too," Sal said.

Dave rubbed his cheek and looked at me. "You think I have a shot?"

"Truth?"

"Wouldn't have it any other way."

"The smart money says no. The DA has been waiting years to nail you for a major crime. Doesn't matter if you did it or not."

He grinned. "Yeah. But I have something going for me he doesn't."

"And that is?"

"You."

5

"I've got a present for you," Luce said, pulling a file folder out of her handbag.

We were at a tiny Asian lunch buffet joint near Times Square. The restaurant was wedged between one of the few remaining Triple X video stores and a souvenir store specializing in fake ivory carvings and electronics that quit working a couple days after you brought them home. It occurred to me both establishments were in the business of selling simulations of the real thing.

"The ME's report?"

"And something else. The tox report."

It had taken her all of a day to snag them.

"What about dental records?"

"Nothing yet."

"Not surprised. Have to be real lucky."

"Luck works for me."

"Can I see the reports?"

"Not so fast. You call me. Say you need a favor. And I drop everything. Then you sweet-talk me with visions of a great lunch." She looked around and made a face. "They should issue biohazard suits at the door."

She wasn't far wrong. The wallboard was pus green, the tape around the joints was peeling, and the hot tables were filled with gummy-looking resinous stuff that defied description.

"You can't always go with first impressions."

"Yeah, I can," she said. "So before we talk business, how about some pleasantries?"

"Fine. How are you?"

"Great, until I walked in here."

"Good. Now can I see the reports?"

She sighed. "You never surprise, Jackson."

Luce was the only person on the planet who called me by my given name.

She slid the file folder across the table.

"They cover the three on the main floor, and the six in the basement," she said.

I read the ME's findings on the squatters first.

Two men. Early twenties. A woman somewhat younger. Soot in their mouths, throats, and lungs. Organs bright cherry red. Meaning elevated levels of carbon monoxide in their blood and tissues. Ditto for cocaine. Even if they'd had time to escape, the combination of CO and cocaine would have made it impossible. They'd died in the fire.

The men in the basement were a different story.

No soot. No carbon monoxide. But the shocker was multiple stab wounds to the groin. Bled out. Dead before the fire hit. Cause of death: homicide.

I moved on to the tox report.

"Rohypnol?" I said.

"Appears so."

"Why use a date rape drug on men?"

"Very good question," Luce said.

"Are roofies part of the gay scene?"

"As a card-carrying lesbian, I never saw roofies. Hell, places I used to frequent folks don't need knockout drugs to get somebody into bed with them."

The germ of an idea began to form.

"Now it's my turn," I said, handing her Sal Lomascio's file. "The findings of the insurance company investigator. Save the prose for later. Look at the photos."

She spread them out on the table and looked away.

"Been doing this a long time and it's still hard to take," she said.

"Forget about the three on the main floor for now. What do you see in the basement?"

"Six rectangles of charcoal," she said.

"The crates are lined up next to each other in two columns of three. Nice and neat. And that says thinking and planning."

"I agree."

"Somehow the doer got these guys to the warehouse. Used Rohypnol as a restraint. And the stab wounds to the groin introduce a sexual element. All in all, very organized."

"Organized to a point," Luce said. "The stab wounds indicate frenzy."

"Right. The doer makes a plan, nabs the guys, and then loses it."

"Classic serial profile. Though a little disorganized at the end."

"Hold that thought," I said.

"OK. If it is a serial killer, the odds say it's likely a Caucasian male between the ages of eighteen and thirty-two who showed signs of abuse as a child. And the sexual element puts a gay man into play."

"A moment ago you said that Rohypnol is rare in the gay scene."

"I did. But that don't mean it's not around. Hell, you can buy anything on the street."

"Fair enough. But if it is a serial, the ages of the vics pose a problem."

"How so?"

"The autopsy gave approximate ages. These guys range from their early forties to sixty plus. Serials typically fantasize about a certain type. The guys in the packing crates are all over the place. Early middle age to considerably older."

"Doesn't really add up, does it?" Luce said.

"It could if we take conventional wisdom off the table."

"How so?"

"Let's say fantasy had nothing to do with it. Maybe the doer was someone with an orderly mind and smart enough to plan things out, but something else was in play."

Luce considered that for a few moments.

"Such as?" she asked

"Revenge. Payback. Any number of things. The groin work and the age range of the men suggests a seriously pissed off prostitute."

"Like Aileen Wuornos, the hooker down in Florida who took out her johns."

"And that's what I'm going with until I find out more about these guys. Like what they had in common."

"And then your theory changes."

"Facts on the ground trump theories any day of the week. In this business you've got to be nimble."

"Or the things that go bump in the night get you before you get them."

"Bingo! Now let's talk about good stuff. How's Cherise?"

Cherise Adams, a Brooklyn cop, was Luce's life partner.

"Just dandy. We're thinking about adopting a child. Got a lawyer who specializes in that kind of thing. We're looking in China, Eastern Europe, south of the border. Anywhere there's a kid who needs a home. Got our fingers crossed."

"Wish you luck, kiddo. You and Cherise would make great parents."

"How about you, Steeg? I always figured you and Ginny for children. Look at the way you take care of DeeDee."

Ginny was my ex-wife, and now a fading memory.

"Not Ginny's fault. She wanted them. I was the problem."

"How so?"

So much for happy stuff.

"Truth?" I said.

"Always a good place to start."

"I was afraid I would turn into my father," I said.

She looked surprised.

"Dominic?" she said.

"An old school cop, and an old school father. Except for the occasional kick in the ass, he kind of left me alone. Dave was the object of his attention."

"I could see how they wouldn't get along," she said.

I was getting tired of having to explain my brother.

"You think he was what he is today when he was a child?"

"I just assumed—"

"He was a kid who wore the mark of Cain on his face. A target for all the little assholes in the Kitchen. Instead of protecting Dave, Dominic piled on."

"Why would he do that?"

"Who the hell knows? What I do know is my brother's first day in my father's house was his best day. After that Dominic turned him into his personal piñata."

"I never knew."

"No reason you should. My turn with Dominic came when I was suspended."

A couple of years ago I clocked a sergeant and wound up doing three months without pay.

"The asshole deserved it," Luce said. "He gave up your snitch."

"He did. But remember, Dominic was an old-school cop. It was bad form to kick the shit out of your boss."

"What does all this have to do with you and progeny?"

"The Steeg family stain could be generational."

"I'm not following."

I told her about Anthony joining Dave in the family business.

"It's really simple," I said. "The Steegs tend to eat their young."

"I love you, Jackson, but that's truly screwed up."

"My life, and welcome to it."

"And that's why you're trying to clear your brother."

"In a nutshell. Besides, I'm convinced Dave didn't kill those guys in the basement and torch his own warehouse."

"But the DA could still get him on felony murder for the squatters."

"Only if he connects him to the arson. Any developments there?"

"They put a special task force on it and they're all running around busy as little bees. A couple of guys are exploring the possibility that Dave is dealing Rohypnol."

"*Please!*"

"They're reaching, Jackson."

"So," I said, "would it be fair to speculate that the task force is ignoring the prostitute angle?"

"They're sticking with your brother. For now. Look at it as a narrow window of opportunity to work your magic."

What Luce didn't say was that the window could slam shut at any time.

6

Dawn Reposo never caught a break.

She was a few years behind me at Most Precious Blood parochial school and, unlike me, at the head of her class. But academics tend to fall by the wayside when your parents are stone-drunk lowlifes. Dawn dropped out and began a steady slide into drugs and prostitution. After I helped her beat her last soliciting charge, we lost track of each other.

I called an old buddy who worked Vice. He ran her. Said she was on parole. Gave me the name of her PO. I called him, and he gave me her last known address. Hadn't heard from her in over a month, he said. Wasn't even sure she still lived there. Said if she didn't check in soon, it was back to the slam.

I told him I'd relay the message.

The subway ride to the Lower East Side took under fifteen minutes.

The address was a tired four-story building on Houston Street, a few blocks from the East River. A bodega occupied the ground floor. The building's entrance was adjacent to the store.

There weren't any names on the mailboxes.

I walked into the bodega and asked if anyone knew Dawn. The three people waiting to buy lottery tickets ignored me. But the counterman's eyes moved to a heavyset Hispanic guy in a motorcycle jacket and jeans sipping coffee from a paper cup. His face looked like it had been on the losing end of an argument with a bat.

The Hispanic guy gave a slight nod.

I made him for Dawn's pimp.

"Three B," the counterman said.

The pimp sidled up next to me.

"What do you want with Dawny?"

"None of your business," I said.

"Wasn't the answer I was looking for."

His breath smelled of onions.

"Try go fuck yourself."

He spent a few moments factoring in my size and attitude, calculating whether he had a reasonable shot.

I found myself hoping he would conclude that the odds were in his favor.

I have a thing about pimps.

"You a cop?" he finally said.

"Take a hike," I said, brushing past him. I expected I would see him again. Soon.

I left the bodega and climbed three flights of stairs to Dawn's apartment. The walls were festooned with some truly artless graffiti.

I knocked on her door.

A few seconds later I heard a hesitant "Yeah?"

"It's Steeg."

The door opened a crack. Then her face appeared. Dawn had clearly overstayed her time in the business. Her hair was dull and lifeless, and her skin was the color of milk gone bad. The pigeon egg–sized purple lump on her left eyebrow kind of summed up the state of her life.

"It is you," she said, breaking into a smile.

"Can I come in?"

She swung the door open.

"Sure," she said. "Long time no see."

"Long time," I agreed.

The apartment was beyond depressing. A few sticks of mismatched furniture that had probably been scavenged from the street. And no little touches that made it a home.

A young Hispanic woman with red streaks in her hair and letters tattooed on her fingers was slumped on the sofa. Her eyes were open but empty.

"Who's she?" I said.

"Gloria somethin'," she said, with a sneer. "A new member of the family. Thinks she's gonna be bottom bitch."

Gloria shot Dawn the bird and closed her eyes, mumbling, "Rickie's tired of your scraggly ass."

"Piece of work," I said.

"Not worth talking about," Dawn said.

Dawn pulled the belt of a ratty cloth coat tight around her even rattier sweat suit.

"I don't like you seein' me like this," she said.

"It's OK. We're friends, Dawn."

"How'd you find me?"

"Your PO. Said he hadn't heard from you in a while."

"You're here to bust me?"

"Nope. Not a cop anymore."

"Then what brings you here?"

"We'll get to that. What happened to your eye?"

Her fingers moved to her eyebrow. "Had to pee in the middle of the night and walked into a door." She tried for a smile. "Always was clumsy."

"The scumbag I ran into down in the bodega have anything to do with it?"

"Who're you talkin' about?"

"The guy with the scrambled face."

"Rickie? No. He's good. Takes care of me."

"I can see that."

"No. You got it all wrong. We're gonna get married. Gloria ain't gonna last long."

A whore's lie. And we both knew it.

"Maybe I can help. Get you into rehab. Turn things around."

She snorted. "Know how many times I been down that road?"

"Once more won't hurt."

"Won't help either," she said. "Just the way it is. Now that that's out of the way, why're you here?"

"Got a problem you may help with."

I told her about the fire.

"So, Dave's got his dick in a crack."

"In a manner of speaking."

"I always liked him. But how can I help?"

"It's possible the men who were murdered were johns, and the killer was doing some payback."

"Why not? Lots of guys I'd like to ice."

"I'm kind of floundering here, Dawn. Don't have much to go on. If it was a pros, it would be hard for her to keep something like this a secret."

"Hookers do like to talk. Especially when they get over on a weirdo John."

"So, have you heard anything?"

The door flew open, and Rickie sauntered in.

He had a hunting knife in his hand.

"Fuck's goin' on?" he said.

Gloria's eyes opened and fixed on Rickie.

Dawn ran up to him. "Put it away. Steeg's a friend."

"I'm the only friend you got," he said, shoving her aside.

I seriously considered tossing Rickie out the window.

He strolled up to me. "Here's the deal. Don't matter if

you came for snatch, or just to chitchat. Gonna cost the same."

I decided that the window required too much effort. I kicked him in the nuts.

Then I picked up the knife and waited until he was done puking.

"That was for tuning Dawn up," I said. "Lay a hand on her again and I'll fucking erase you."

"Rickie didn't do this to me, Steeg," she said. "He loves me."

I let the *love* bullshit pass without comment.

"Then who did?"

She and Rickie exchanged glances. I had the feeling that he didn't want Dawn to go down that road. But she shrugged him off.

"Same people who did Rickie," Dawn said.

"What does that mean?"

"Somebody looking to take over prostitution in the city. Forcing girls to work for them. And hassling pimps who push back."

"Hell of a business model."

"Came after me a few nights ago. I was working the Lincoln Tunnel and this guy lays it out for me. Sell my ass for him, or get hurt. I tell him to fuck off, and he pops me. Rickie sees what's happening and goes for the guy."

I looked over at Rickie. He still hadn't got his sea legs yet.

"Because he loves you," I said.

She let that slide.

"Do you want to hear what happened or not?"

Not really. I had zero interest in getting involved in a war between lowlifes. But Dawn was determined to tell her story, so I let her.

"Sure," I said.

"It's been going on for some time, and all the girls are scared shitless. Afraid to work. Same thing happened to Gloria."

"Did you go to the cops?"

"Like they would give a shit?"

Against my better judgment, I gave her my card.

"If he bothers you again, let me know. Old times' sake."

She jammed the card into her coat pocket.

"About Dave's problem," Dawn said. "There's an outfit you might want to check out."

"Who?"

"No one," Rickie said, glaring at her.

Dawn ignored him.

"Is there a problem?" I said.

"He worries about me. That's all. Anyway, I went to them a while ago. It didn't work out."

"Why's that?"

She shrugged. "It just wasn't right for me."

Apparently, that's about all I was going to get.

"OK."

"It's a foundation, or some shit like that. Called Another Chance. Works with girls trying to get out of the life. Run by Martine Toussaint, an ex-hooker. Haitian. You may know her."

"Doesn't ring a bell. But she's proof there's life after prostitution. Something to think about."

"Please skip the sermon."

"You're right. Another Chance," I said. "I'll look into it."

"Do me a favor."

"Name it."

"Don't mention my name. Martine and I didn't get along. Bad feelings on both sides."

Seemed to be a lot of that going around.

was on my way to Feeney's when Luce called.

"We got lucky with one of the vics in the basement," she said.

"Dental records?"

"Better. Guy had a pacemaker. We tracked the serial number to the hospital, and the doc who did the surgery."

"And?"

"Led us to Martin Donnelly. Wife was interviewed."

"Anything useful?"

"Not really. I spoke to the detectives who met with her. Basic stuff. He was an insurance agent. Loving husband. Coached Little League."

"Sounds like a wonderful guy. But not much."

"Their hearts weren't in it, Jackson."

"Mind if I have a go?"

"Be my guest."

• • •

The Donnellys lived in a stately Tudor in the hilly Field-stone section of the Bronx. Fieldstone was an odd little community filled with judges, politicians, and heavy-duty money, which disavowed all connection to the city, and especially to The Bronx.

I rang the bell.

A few seconds later, Helen Donnelly answered the door with a drink in her hand. She seemed a bit unsteady.

"My name is Steeg," I said, handing her my card. "I'm investigating your husband's murder. Could I have . . . ?"

She barely glanced at the card before slamming the door in my face.

Not a surprising reaction when someone who looks like me shows up on your doorstep.

I rang the bell.

"Mrs. Donnelly? All I need is a few minutes of your time."

Her voice drifted out from behind the door.

"I've already spoken with the police. Piss off!"

"I know you have."

"Then stop bothering me."

I rang the bell again.

It was time to appeal to her softer side.

"An innocent man may go down for his murder."

"Why should I give a damn?"

At this point, most people would have either stopped talking or called the police. But Mrs. Donnelly kept the conversation going. No doubt about it, I was making headway.

"Because it's my brother."

There was silence. As it dragged on, the more my prospects dimmed.

Then she said, "You're still there, aren't you?"

"I am."

"And you're not going away."

"Nope."

"Persistent son of a bitch. Do you drink, Mr. Steeg?"

"Used to."

"Socially, or vocationally?"

"The latter."

"Me too. And still at it. Screw the twelve-step tango."

The door swung open. "What the hell," she said. "Come on in. Could use the company."

First time alcoholism ever worked for me, I thought.

Helen Donnelly was a tall, attractive woman in her early forties. The little makeup she wore was expertly applied.

She led me to an L-shaped sofa in the living room, ordered me to sit, and perched herself two cushions away. A half-empty bottle of Cristal sat on the coffee table.

"Tell me again," she said, refilling her glass. "What's your interest in Martin's death?"

Her cheeks were boozy pink, but her speech was tight and controlled.

"I'm a private investigator. My brother's been accused of your husband's death. Wrongfully, I believe."

She emptied her glass. "The police said they had a suspect." Her lips curled into a wry smile. "Thought it would comfort me."

"Does it?"

She smoothed the front of her pearl gray silk blouse.

"Remains to be seen. So, if the police think your brother is guilty, why do you believe otherwise?"

"Ownership of a warehouse is not de facto evidence of murder. And it's the only thing they have that links him to the crime."

She considered that for a moment.

"Is he a good man?" she finally said.

"Yes, though not without faults."

She looked out at the patio. A bird with a dark body and gray belly snacked at a feeder.

"Our faults too often define us," she said, with a resigned shake of her head. "What can I tell you that I haven't shared with the detectives?"

"Sometimes a second telling provides more information. Let's talk about Martin."

Her fingers toyed with a tiny gold crucifix that hung from a thin chain around her neck.

"His death was the most dramatic event of his life."

She caught the surprise in my eyes.

"Not what you expected from the grieving widow, was it?"

Not by a long shot.

"Well, Mr. Steeg, you were honest with me. I'm returning the favor. If your brother is truly innocent, his conviction would be the only sad outcome of this mess."

"Why do you say that?"

"My husband was an unusual man. And not in a good way."

"How so?"

"Except for the Little League team his agency sponsored, Martin was a man of negligible passion, fewer interests, and no friends."

"Even you?"

"Especially me."

She took a healthy shot of Cristal and smacked her lips. "The man was barely socialized. In or out of bed."

"Did you mention this to the detectives?"

"They never asked. Look, our marriage was like two ships passing in the night. Martin had his life, and I had mine. Connections were few and far between."

"Any children?"

"Fortunately, no."

"Why do you say that?"

She didn't answer. Instead, her gaze wandered back out to the terrace. The bird was gone.

"Were there other women?"

A faintly bitter smile played on her lips.

She got up from the sofa. "I'm very tired, Mr. Steeg," she said. "I hope you got what you came for."

I sensed I had something, but I wasn't sure exactly what.

8

Nick D'Amico sat at one end of the bar drinking coffee from a chipped mug. A woman sat at the other end of the bar working her way through eggs over easy and hash browns. She looked vaguely familiar.

I sidled up to Nick and took a seat on a stool.

"What're the chances of getting something to eat?" I said

"Zip, unless you want to cook it yourself."

"What's the problem?"

"Julio, the stickup artist masquerading as my cook, got busted again."

"So? It isn't the first time. Call his brother."

"He's in the slam too. Something about playing fast and loose with an ice pick. Guy owed him some money and he got tired of waiting."

"Anyone else in the family knows how to work a griddle?"

"The better question is whether anyone else in the family knows how to work."

I jerked my chin in the direction of the woman at the end of the bar.

"Where'd she get her meal?"

"I ordered in," Nick said. "You want something, the deli is two doors up."

"Why does she rate?"

"Another sad story in a neighborhood filled with them. Name's Stella Tedesco. You probably know her daughter, Jenny Tyler."

"The actress?"

"That's the one. Mostly a bit player who got lucky. A featured role in a movie with Nicholson last year. Critics said she was great. I thought she sucked. But what do I know? Anyway, Stella has been supporting Jenny and her bum boyfriends for years. Ran through all her money. And now when the daughter is about to make it big, she doesn't even know her. Should've drowned her at birth."

"Compassion isn't your style."

"Nothing to do with it. My kids ain't gonna let no senior citizen residence suck away what's left of my money."

"You're being paranoid."

"Really? They want to know where my will is stashed. Where I got the safety deposit boxes. The whole megillah."

"Maybe they're just being prudent."

"Yeah? Well they ain't gonna get shit. Let 'em work for it like I did." He glanced over at Stella Tedesco. "She never asked for nothing, and what did it get her?"

"A meal on you."

"Fuck it!" he said. "What're you doing here so early?"

"The boiler died again. So I figured I'd come here for some warmth and good feelings."

"One out of two ain't bad."

"What's going on with my brother? I haven't heard from him in a few days."

"He's back to being a fucking hermit. But Anthony is another story. Strutting around like the cock of the walk. Him and that mope Tommy Cisco. The Masters of Crime. Every time you look at them, they're huddled together hatching schemes." He made a face. "Those two couldn't plan a decent purse snatch."

"Maybe Dave figures that Anthony'll bring some advanced business techniques gleaned from the Ivy League."

"Yeah, that'll work."

"Oh, ye of little faith."

The door swung open. My nephew and Tommy Cisco blew in on the breeze.

"My day is complete," Nick said. "Bonnie and Clyde are in the house."

"Hey, Uncle Jake, how're you doing?" Anthony said. A big smile was pasted to his face.

I called his smile with a glare.

"In the pink," I said.

"Glad I found you. Tommy here would like to straighten things out between you. You know, no bad blood going forward."

I turned to Cisco. Just over the bridge of his nose he had a large purple welt like a third eye, encircled by a pretty pale blue corona.

He held out his hand.

I ignored it.

"Listen, Steeg. I was a little out of line the other day, and I just want you to know there're no hard feelings."

"Am I supposed to give a shit?"

It wasn't the answer he was expecting. His hand sort of drifted down to his thigh.

"Now," I said, "do me a favor and take a walk while I talk to my nephew."

Cisco threw Anthony a look like he was asking permission.

"It's OK, Tommy," Anthony said. "This won't take long."

Cisco nodded and did a slow amble toward the front. When he reached the door, I grabbed a handful of Anthony's coat and drag-walked him to the kitchen.

"What's your *problem*?" he said, rearranging his clothes.

"Cut the Tony Soprano act. It doesn't fit. What the hell is going on with you?"

His face reddened.

"I don't know what you're talking about."

"I'm the one guy who actually gives a shit what happens to you."

"You're forgetting about my father."

"He's too busy worrying about *his* future to give a shit about yours."

"You don't know shit. He loves me."

"I'll give you that," I said. "But he's got an odd way of showing it."

He poked a finger in my chest, and his face twisted into a threat. "Don't you fuckin' criticize him! And don't you ever put your hands on me again."

This wasn't the kid I helped raise. The boy I considered my son. Anthony was turning into my brother.

"Right now he needs me," he said.

"When it comes to his business, your father doesn't need anyone."

"Thanks for the advice," he said, turning to go.

"Have you spoken to your mother?"

He stopped and turned around.

His voice was icy. "She had her shot, and left. He needed her and she walked."

"Maybe she needed him and your father came up short."

"Screw you!" he said.

I reached for him. To throw my arms around him and tell him I understood what he was going through. Tell him not to let my brother screw up his life the way Dominic screwed up Dave's.

"Anthony . . ."

I never saw it coming.

There wasn't any pain. Just a shock that started high up on my temple and traveled down to my knees, driving me to the ground.

When I was able to focus, I saw Anthony standing over me. His face was contorted with rage.

"I warned you," he said. "Don't you ever put your hands on me again."

9

Another Chance was housed in a brownstone on the Upper East Side. A low, wrought iron fence topped with artichoke finials bounded two tiny snow-covered gardens on either side of the stairway.

At the entrance, a small black sign with white letters instructed me to ring the bell.

I did. A few moments later the door opened. Two burly guys with buzz cuts—one a few inches taller than the other—greeted me.

"What can I do for you?" the taller one said. The skin on his face was steroid-tight.

"I'm here to see Martine Toussaint."

"Got an appointment?"

"Didn't know I needed one."

"Who referred you?"

"No one. Just need to ask her a few questions."

"About what?"

This was getting tiresome.

I gave him my card. "Tell her I'd like a few minutes of her time."

He glanced at the card. "She know you?"

"Just do it," I said.

He considered that for a few seconds. "Wait here," he finally said.

The door closed.

A few minutes later he was back.

"She'll see you."

"Terrific."

The reception area was small but comfortably furnished. The recessed lighting in the ceiling bathed the room in a muted glow. Shorter Guy sat on the arm of a sofa and eyed me as we passed through.

I followed Tall Guy down a short corridor to Martine Toussaint's office. The best word to describe it was *sleek*.

Hardwood floor buffed to a high shine, chrome-and-leather furniture, modern art on the walls. Martine, a dreadlocked beauty with skin the color of cocoa, sat behind a glass-topped desk dealing out a hand of tarot cards.

My first impression was that there was a hell of a disconnect between Martine Toussaint's digs and her charitable work.

She laid the cards down and stood up.

"Steeg," she said, with a smile. "Come in."

"You want me to sit in?" Tall Guy said.

"Not necessary, Frank. Mr. Steeg is an acquaintance. Although it's obvious he doesn't remember me."

She was right. I didn't.

"OK," Frank said. "I'll be out front if you need me."

"Help me out here, Martine," I said. "How do we know each other?"

"You're a cop in Hell's Kitchen. I was a whore in the same place. We know the same people."

"And they would be?"

"Dawn Reposo, for one."

I nodded. "She worked the neighborhood."

"And all the girls envied her."

"Why's that?"

"You were her personal Get Out of Jail Free card. Wish I had an angel on my shoulder like you." She paused. "Seen her lately?"

"No. Think of her every now and again, though."

"Why the visit?"

"I'll get to that. How'd you manage to wind up here?"

She gathered the cards up, shuffled them, and, one by one, laid them out on the desktop.

"Long story, Steeg. Let's just say I got righteous. And used the brains God gave me."

"Now you're helping other girls get just as righteous."

Her gaze drifted to the tarot cards, lingered for a few moments, and then shifted back to me.

"Doing God's work," she said.

I looked around the office.

"He's certainly showered his bounty on you."

"One thing I learned on the streets. He helps those who help themselves."

"Looks to me like you helped yourself just fine."

"Another Chance is a nonprofit organization. I couldn't have launched it without financial support from several important people who think the sex trade is an abomination."

"Like those two worthies outside?"

"You mean Frank Ennis and John Riley?"

"The only guys out in your waiting room."

"They work for me."

"Doing what?"

"This is dangerous work, Steeg. Whenever a girl accepts our help, her life—my life—is in danger from pimps who just lost a source of income."

"How many girls do you work with?"

"Anywhere from twenty to thirty at a time. We provide them with safe housing, peer counseling, drug rehab, vocational training, and money to get them started."

"And Ennis and Riley."

She gathered the cards together and set them aside.

"So, the reason for the visit?" she said.

"I'm working a case. Privately. Looking for a prostitute who feels abused enough to commit murder."

"And you came here?"

"Just to develop a few leads. Hoping you might help."

She looked down at the deck of cards and then back at me.

"My job is to protect these girls. And we do that by

promising them confidentiality. Besides, you're not going to get anywhere with them. Hookers lie."

"So you're saying . . . ?"

She picked up the deck, fanned it out on the desktop, and examined it closely.

"It's not in the cards."

10

The Majestic Hotel was a relic of a time when the Bowery was the last stop on the train ride to perdition. Four stories of misery for folks who dove into the bottle and never came out.

I could have been one of them. For years I had been riding Johnny Black's one-trick pony, until it occurred to me it was better to change mounts.

A small group of the curious and just plain bored clustered behind yellow police tape watching the action. I gave a uniform my name and told him Luce Guidry was expecting me. He disappeared into the hotel. A few minutes later he reappeared and waved me in.

Luce, along with a bunch of cops and techs trying to look useful, was in what passed for the lobby—a small, dingy space sporting a counter with a Plexiglas partition, ceiling-high gates, and no chairs for the weary. It had the pungent smell of puke and body odor.

"What've you got?" I said.

Luce wrinkled her nose and looked around.

"How do they live like this?" she said.

"Not too many options."

"Cubicles so small they would cramp an elf. Mangy cots filled with mangier people. And vermin for bedmates."

She gave a despairing shake of her head.

"Sometimes, Jackson, the human condition just gets me down. Anyway, I got something you might be interested in."

"And that would be?"

"Another stiff," she said. "Want a peek?"

I followed her through an opening in the gate and into a rear office. The lower drawer of the room's lone filing cabinet—about five feet wide and three drawers high—was pulled out. Its original contents had been scattered on the floor and replaced by a body. He looked to be middle-aged. Except for a tonsure of black hair going to gray, he was bald. Large freckles dotted his scalp.

On the linoleum just under the drawer lay an amoeba-shaped pool of blood.

"Hell of a filing system," I said. "Meticulous to a fault."

"Even managed to file him under the M's."

"And why would this gentleman be of interest to me?"

"Could be one of yours."

"You're being very elliptical here."

"Another stabbing victim. Especially, down low. Seeing a heap of that lately."

"And you're going to have the ME do a tox screen to see if there are roofies in his blood."

"As soon as they get here and cart him off. Seems this is a busy day at the morgue. Shooting up in Harlem. A couple of domestics where things really got out of hand. And an old guy lost control of his car and took out a flea market in SoHo. Bodies were flying like Frisbees."

"The day goes faster when you're busy. Have you had a chance to look at the tapes from the hotel's security cameras?"

"You're kidding, right? When you get seven, eight bucks a night, and for guests you got zombies with first-run showings of DTs playing in their heads, are you gonna put your money into videotape?"

Fair point.

"Any witnesses?"

"Yeah. Three monkeys. Hear no evil, speak no evil, and the ever popular see no evil."

"How about the guy who runs the counter? The manager. Did he notice anyone come in with the vic?"

"He is the vic."

"Fancy that."

"Name's Cady. Walter Cady."

"The clues just keep on coming."

"And we have something else," Luce said. "His computer. Which has already been bagged and tagged, and is on the way to Forensics. Never know what those curious little data miners may dig up."

"And, of course, you'll keep me posted."

"It's what I live for, Jackson. By the way, how's Dee Dee?"

"Got a boyfriend. Justin Hapner."

"The beginning of a lifetime of complications."

A cop appeared at the door. He was maybe eighteen, and had the acne to prove it.

"Detective Guidry?" he said. "Hate to bother you. The body baggers are here."

"Much as I'd like to spend the rest of the day chitchatting with you, Jackson, unlike you I've got work to do. Oh, I almost forgot. We found another one that could be yours."

"You're kidding."

"Found him in a room in that grubby little hotel on the West Side that's kinda shaped like a rhombus. Stabbed. In that special place."

"Did you get his name off the hotel registry?"

"Yeah. Millard Fillmore."

"Any witnesses?"

"In a hot bed joint? Please! But we'll run his prints and see what turns up."

The murders were tumbling into each other. Not much space between them. It was as if the killer was working herself into a frenzy. And having a hard time keeping it together.

Luce and I parted company in the street. The crowd

outside the flophouse had thinned to just a few people waiting for the final act before they got on with their day. One of them, an old, disheveled guy with a faded tattoo creeping up his neck, disengaged himself from the small knot of people and walked up to me.

"Got a buck for an old-timer who's seen it all?" he said.

The bridge of his nose was flattened. And his eyes were hooded under two thick plates of old scar tissue that sat on what used to be his eyebrows.

I reached into my pocket and handed him a five.

"What's your name, my friend?" I said.

"They call me Sailor."

"So, what have you seen, Sailor?" I said.

"Things that get into your head and don't let go."

"I'm familiar with the experience."

He grinned. "Most folks are, but don't admit it."

I jerked my chin at the Majestic.

"You live there?" I said.

He rubbed the five-dollar bill between his thumb and forefinger. "Reckon I will tonight. Once the commotion dies down."

"Where did you fight?"

With the pads of his fingers he gently stroked the scar tissue jutting out above his right eye.

"Wherever there was a payday," he said. "Don't recollect much about it. Think I was good, though." He looked at my face, and then took my hand and studied my oversized, battered knuckles. "Looks like you worked the canvas some."

"Amateurs."

"Counts," he said, releasing my hand. "Hurts as much whether they pay you or not."

I was developing an affection for Sailor.

I pulled out a card and tucked it into his jacket pocket.

"Hold on to that. If you get jammed up, I'm someone to call."

He nodded.

"You knew Walter Cady?" I said.

"Never knew Walter had a last name. Much less one that was so highfalutin'."

"What can you tell me about him?"

"Kept to himself mostly. Invisible. Like everyone else who lives on the skids."

"Any family?"

"If he had, he never talked about them."

"Friends? Anyone close?"

"Ain't no one's your friend down here. Take the coins off a dead man's eyes and buy a shot."

"Cady like to hit the bottle every now and again? Maybe do a little blow?"

Sailor rubbed his chin and thought on it a bit.

"Don't rightly know. He wasn't the kind of guy who gave much away."

"Big with the ladies?"

He smiled as if replaying a memory.

"Not fittin' to speak ill of the dead," he said.

He jammed his fists in his pockets and turned to walk away.

"Where're you off to now, Sailor?"

"Don't rightly know. But I know where I'm hopin' to wind up."

"Where's that?"

"Big Rock Candy Mountain," he said. "Sure to find old Walt waitin' for me."

11

I hopped a B train and rode it to Times Square. From there I walked over to Feeney's.

On my way, I passed Benny Kim's store. He wasn't at his usual spot stripping rose petals. Strange. I went into the store and found Mrs. Kim behind the cash register. Her face was lined with worry.

"Everything all right, Mrs. Kim?"

"No."

"Anything I can do?"

"Go away!"

"Where's Benny?"

"In back. In office. Leave him alone. He don't want to see anyone."

"What happened?"

"Nothing. Just go."

I went into the back. The smell of rotting vegetables hung in the air like a miasma.

Benny sat at his desk poring over receipts. His right eye was blackened, and a lump the size of a peach poked out of his forehead.

"Talk to me, Benny," I said.

"Go away."

"Who did this to you?"

"Karma."

"Karma?"

"Sins in other lives jump up and bite me in the ass."

"We've all got a lot to atone for, my friend. But it wasn't karma who did the actual punching."

"You don't want to know."

"Actually, I do."

After some gentle prodding he told me.

Feeney's didn't do much of a late afternoon business. The serious drinking started early in the morning and tapered off until the sun went down. Then it picked up again after dinner, with a vengeance.

When I arrived, the Closed sign was on the door. But I could make out the action through the window.

A heavyset guy with black sideburns and blood streaming down his face was on all fours. Nick, gripping a folding chair above his head, loomed over him. He brought the chair down on the poor bastard's back with enough force to flatten a bull elephant.

I slammed the flat of my hand against the plate glass of the door.

It got Nick's attention.

He dropped the chair, strolled to the door, and unlocked it.

"What in hell are you doing?" I said.

"Doc said I needed some exercise," Nick said.

"Who is this guy?"

"Used to be one of my workers until he figured he could short me and get away with it."

"How about just firing him?"

"Object lesson. Guinea works the Brooklyn docks. Longshoreman. A liquor shipment came in a few days ago. Scotch. Brandy. High-priced shit."

"Not the stuff you sell here."

"Not even close. Headed for that la-di-dah liquor store on Fifth. I was supposed to get five cases. Wound up with four."

"Your workout ends here."

Nick's voice was low and his eyes had a psycho sparkle. "I don't tell you how to handle your business, and you don't tell me how to handle mine."

"This time I do," I said.

Nick walked up to me so close I could count the bits of gray stubble on his cheeks.

"Don't fuck with me, Steeg. Not in the mood."

I didn't move.

"Makes two of us," I said.

After a few seconds of mulling things over and weighing the odds, Nick backed away.

I helped the guy to his feet and told him to make tracks. He mumbled his thanks and wobbled out the door.

The sound of quiet applause came from a booth in the back.

My brother was in the house.

"Nicely done, Jake," he said. "The Righter of Wrongs has struck again."

"Good to see you finally came out of the attic and rejoined the world."

He slid out of the booth and walked up to me.

"It was *my* booze," he said.

"Since when did beating someone to death become your spectator sport of choice, Dave? I remember when you did your own dirty work."

His eyes went flat.

"What's bothering you, Jake?"

"You and your kid."

His eyes, still flat, squinted slightly at the corners.

"What's that supposed to mean?" he said.

"I just had an interesting little chat with Benny Kim."

"The slant fruit guy?"

"The Korean businessman."

"Whatever."

"Seems that there's been a rash of car heists in the neighborhood lately."

"So? What's that got to do with me . . . or Anthony?"

"Anthony and the chimpanzee who works for him drive up to Bennie's store in Bennie's car. Anthony sits in the car while the monkey goes in and lays it out for Benny. He wants his car back, it's gonna cost him. Benny tells him to fuck himself. The monkey takes umbrage and kicks the shit out of him."

Dave stroked the pebbled patch on his cheek.

"Boys'll be boys."

"You set the rules a long time ago, Dave: Lay off the locals; you take care of them, they take care of you. Well, these guys are local. Live in the neighborhood."

He smiled and patted me on the cheek.

"Your problem is you take things too seriously," he said.

"Or maybe the direction your life has taken has screwed up your brain."

"Don't go there."

"If not me, who?"

"He's my son."

"But he's not you," I said.

"That remains to be seen."

12

The more I thought about it, the less I liked about Martine Toussaint's story.

A twenty-buck-a-pop streetwalker climbs the greasy pole out of prostitution. Then, like Saint Paul on the Road to Damascus, she has an epiphany. And devotes her life to helping working girls go straight. Then she convinces a bunch of rich guys to come along for the ride. With nothing but good works on their minds, they front the money. Enough to pay for a brownstone and a lifestyle Martine could only dream of when she was selling her body at the tunnels.

What it had to do with Dave, I didn't know. But it didn't add up.

The clerk at the lower Broadway office of the Attorney General's Charities Bureau was deep into a conversation on her cell phone. Something about a rat bastard named

Tony who wasn't going to get away with whatever the hell he had done . . . a second time.

"Excuse me," I said.

She threw me a disgusted look and showed me her back.

About a minute later she swiveled her head around and, discovering I was still there, said into the phone, "I gotta go now."

Then she turned to me.

"*What?*"

"I need some information about a charity," I said.

"Which one?"

"Another Chance."

"Secular or religious?"

"Does it make a difference?"

She sighed as if it were her lot in life to suffer fools and their equally stupid questions.

"Only secular charities are required to register with the attorney general," she said.

I doubted whether Another Chance was an arm of the Church of the Holy Tarot.

"Let's go with secular."

"Another Chance," she said, typing it into her computer.

She stared at the screen.

"Nothing," she said. "Anything else?"

"Try Martine Toussaint." I spelled her name.

"Zip," she said. "Are we done?"

"Yep. And you can tell Tony for me he really blew it. You're a catch!"

The lobby of the apartment house directly across the street offered a perfect view of the comings and goings at Martine's brownstone.

The snow was pounding, the wind was swirling, and the temperature was in the teens.

The doorman stood in the vestibule. He was a big man with a thatch of neatly combed white hair, wearing a Gilbert and Sullivan costume. The epaulets of his red greatcoat were trimmed in gold. He held the matching cap loosely in his fingers and away from his body, as if wearing it would be the ultimate insult. I made him for a retired cop picking up a few bucks working the door.

"Can I help you?" he said.

"Looking for some information," I said.

He jerked his chin at the door. "Take a walk."

I handed him my card.

His gaze moved from the card and back to me. "I used to know a Steeg. Detective. Midtown North."

"Dominic. My father."

"That's the one," he said. "How's he doing?"

"Passed away. Two years ago."

"Sorry to hear that. Good cop."

Actually he wasn't, but there was no point to opening that can of worms.

"That's what they say."

"Yeah. I heard one of his kids was on the force, and the other was a bad apple."

"The cop would be me."

He waggled the card in my face. "Not what it says here."

"Things change."

He nodded. "Know how that goes. Figured I would retire and live good on the pension. And now I'm dressed up like a fucking Russian general and opening doors for people who lost the ability to do it on their own."

"Not the way you thought it would be."

"Not the way it ought to be," he said. "So, what can I do for Dominic's kid?"

"That brownstone across the street. Another Chance. Know anything about it?"

"What's your interest?"

"Working a case."

He smiled. "You got my juices flowing."

"So what can you tell me?"

"Popular place."

"How so?"

"Double-parked limos. Guys in suits that cost more than my rent."

"Anyone you recognize?"

He gave me some names. A congressman. A couple of state senators. A judge. And my very own councilman, Terry Sloan. The asshole!

"Very public-spirited gentlemen," I said.

"That's one way of looking at it."

"Very cynical. What's your take on what's going on?"

"There was a time when I would have been interested. Now all I want is to hang on to this job."

A cab pulled up.

He ambled to the door. "I gotta get back to work."

As I followed him out, my gaze drifted to Martine's brownstone across the street. Frank Ennis stood on the top of the stairs with his arms folded across his chest.

Seems I was the object of his attention.

13

Terry Sloan looked up from his BlackBerry, saw me standing at his office door, and the blood drained from his face.

He jammed the BlackBerry into his jacket pocket.

"What in hell are you doing here?"

I took that as an invitation to walk in.

Councilman Terry Sloan and I had a spotty relationship. Actually, that was an understatement. We loathed each other.

I had a problem with slimebags who rode political office to the pot of gold at the end of the rainbow. And he had a problem with me playing his Greek chorus. But Terry was a plugged-in guy, and there was little that went on in the city that escaped his attention. Especially if there was big money involved.

Martine Toussaint nagged at me like a bad tooth.

Maybe she really was doing the Lord's work. Or maybe she was running a scam and didn't want me gumming up the works. Or maybe the truth—an interesting word full of tricky shades and meanings—was far different, and had something to do with what I was after.

So far, Terry was my best shot at narrowing the possibilities.

"Trying to save Dave's hash," I said, "and figured you might be able to help."

"After what he did to me?"

He had a point. Terry and my brother were once real close. But in a completely psychotic moment, Dave drove a fork into Sloan's thigh for not showing me the proper respect.

"Yeah, but think about what he's done *for* you," I said.

"That doesn't give him the right—"

"Yeah, it does. Comes with the Faustian bargain of doing business with Dave."

"Bullshit! I still walk with a limp."

If he was looking for sympathy, I was fresh out.

"Small price to pay, Terry. Let's be honest. God gave you the brains of your average macaw. But thanks to Dave you're living the lush life."

Terry jumped up from behind the desk, positively vibrating.

"You don't know shit about what I went through to get where I am. Now, get the fuck out of here, or I'll have you thrown out."

"Why not start with the piece of the carting business

Dave gave you? Or the kickbacks from the developers. Or the ridiculous interest on the hundred large you have on the street. Oh, and let's not forget your sweetheart arrangement with the longshoreman's union. Can't have any of that getting out, can we?"

Terry went white.

"How do you . . . ?"

"I'm Dave's brother, you moron."

"Are you threatening me?"

"Sure."

The air went out of him.

"Whattya want?"

"Martine Toussaint."

A fine sheen of sweat appeared on his forehead.

"What do you want with her?"

"I hear you know her."

"From who?"

"One of your many admirers."

"Fuck you, Steeg!"

"Let's get back to Martine."

"Runs a charity for hookers," he said.

"She legit?"

"Fucked if I know."

"Now, Terry, we both know better than that."

"Why're you interested in her?"

"Dave's legal problems."

"You think she set the fire?"

"No. But for now she's a person of interest for the murders of the men in the basement."

"That's not her business, Steeg."

"Then what is?"

"Walk away. Best advice I can give."

He came around his desk, took my arm, and nudged me to the door.

I held my ground.

"Why?"

"There's a set of words that old mapmakers used for really dangerous spots on the ocean."

"And they would be?"

"Here be dragons."

"You're being very elliptical, Terry."

"Stay away from her," he said. "I'm serious, Steeg, it's the best advice I can give you."

"Can't do that."

He shrugged. "Then it's on you."

"What's she running out of that brownstone?"

He flashed me a cold smile.

"You never learn, do you?" he said.

"Actually, I did learn something. You're more frightened of the lady than the tiger."

"Or maybe I'm just a piece of plankton at the end of the food chain."

"First time I've heard you admit that you're small-time," I said.

"When the elephants dance, you gotta be nimble."

Could be Terry was smarter than I'd thought.

14

The Hampstead was a no-star hotel near One Police Plaza. The price was right, the appointments minimal, and that made it the go-to place to stash witnesses and other people of interest to the NYPD.

I was there because the girl who'd died in the fire had been identified. A runaway named Angela Klemper. Her parents had come to New York to identify her body and take her home.

Luce was going to interview them and invited me along.

She was wearing a dark pantsuit, low heels, and in a shocking departure, a few selected pieces of artful jewelry.

"I see you're in confidence-building mode," I said.

"More like I'm draped in widow's weeds," she said. "But nothing says trust better than your basic black."

"How'd you manage to arrange my presence?"

"You're a special consultant working with the police department to help find the people who murdered their daughter."

"Never been a consultant before. How much does it pay?"

That drew a loud snort.

"And here I was hoping to make a killing," I said.

"Bad choice of words. These people have been through the mill today, Jackson, they're kind of skittish. So go easy."

"What're they like?"

"Jonas and Adele. Mother's mousy and doesn't say much. Jonas seems to run the show. Major piece of work."

"How so?"

"His daughter was reduced to a cinder, and he's the aggrieved party."

"Why am I not surprised?"

The hotel room was about as I'd expected—queen-sized bed, two end tables, couple of chairs, a non-widescreen TV bolted to a dresser made out of pressboard, and a print of a bucolic glen over the bed. Days Inn without the charm.

The Kemplers sat on the bed with their backs to each other. An interesting bit of body language. But, given the circumstances, understandable. Grief tends to strip the gears of life.

Adele Klemper was a big-boned woman in a shapeless dark dress. She had dull, bovine eyes, and picked at a scab on her cheek with a fingernail. Jonas wore rumpled beige corduroy slacks and a bulky brown sweater. His face was fleshy and unshaven, and his close-cropped black hair was peppered with gray.

The television was on. An infomercial promoting a set of knives that could, with a mere few swipes, reduce two-inch-thick steel plate to a pile of shavings seemed to have Jonas's attention. It had mine, too. I made a mental note to check it out the next time I needed to saw a bowling ball in half.

Luce made the introductions.

From then on, things pretty much went downhill.

Jonas Klemper turned his attention away from the TV and on to me.

"Had enough bullshit today," he said. "Don't need more from you."

"Mr. Klemper, I'm truly sorry for your loss. And I promise I'm not going to take up more than a few minutes of your time."

"You gonna bring my baby back?"

"I wish I could. But I'll do my level best to find the person who did this to her. Just a few questions and I'll be on my way."

"Screw your questions. I want answers. And so far all I'm getting is bullshit from you people."

"Jonas," Adele said. "He means well, just—"

He whirled around.

"Damn it, Adele. Don't you go telling me what to do. Weren't for you, none of this would have happened."

Adele's eyes briefly registered a spark of fear. And then went blank. I had the feeling she had been through this before. She lowered her head and turned her attention back to the scab.

The combination of Jonas's posturing and Adele's retreat told me that nothing useful would come of this. It was time to separate them.

I put a friendly hand on Jonas's shoulder and nudged him toward the door.

"Luce, Jonas and I are heading down to the bar. Why don't you stay with Adele until we get back. Won't be long. That OK with you, Jonas?"

Luce gave me a slight nod and sat down next to Adele and took her hand.

Jonas threw his wife an angry look. "Why not? Being cooped up here with her is making me buggy anyway."

The bar was empty. We settled in at a corner table. I ordered a Diet Coke. Jonas went for a beer.

"Not normally a drinking man," he said. "But you lose your two girls, it kinda does something to you."

Two daughters? I was confused.

"You lost two girls?"

"First, Wanda. And now Angela."

"How did Wanda die?"

"Didn't die. Least as far as I know. She ran."

I filed that away for later.

"What do you do for a living, Jonas?"

"Trucker. Farm some a little on the side. Work my ass off for my family."

"Bet you do. Not easy working two jobs."

He tipped the glass to his mouth and drained it, using the sleeve of his sweater to blot the foam off his lips.

"Damn straight," he said. "Thankless. Thankless as a son of a bitch."

"Adele work too?"

"No sir. I believe in old-fashioned values."

I flashed him a smile. "You don't see much of that anymore."

"And it's a shame," Jonas said. "Woman's place is in the home. Raising the kids. Making sure there's a hot supper waiting when you come home. There can only be one master of the house."

"Right from the Good Book. Read it every day," I said. "Keep it right on my bedside table."

I was fully expecting lightning to strike. But not before Jonas had fully warmed up.

"World would be better for it, if more people followed your example. All the wisdom you ever need."

"Couldn't agree with you more. So, tell me about Angela."

He tapped the empty glass. "You think I can get a refill?"

"No problem," I said, signaling the waiter.

Less than a minute passed before his beer arrived.

When it did, he knocked it right back the same as the first.

"Where were we?" he said.

"Angela."

"Right. My baby started off just fine. Not like her sister."

"How so?"

"Wanda was willful. Headstrong. Didn't mind her daddy."

"But Angela was different."

"Oh yeah. Sweet little thing. Did what she was supposed to. Never gave me a moment's trouble."

"What changed her?"

"Wanda," he said. "Set a bad example. Pretty soon, Angela was acting like her sister."

"And what was Wanda doing?"

"Boys were sniffing around her like dogs in heat. And she was Johnny-on-the-spot. You know how that goes."

"I can see where that would be a problem."

"Was. And Adele just coddled them."

"And you had to lay down the law."

"Sure did. Spare the rod, spoil the child."

"Did Adele need disciplining too?"

Jonas signaled for another beer.

He nodded. "She had to learn to do right."

I could feel a bubble of heat rising from down deep inside of me.

"Has Adele figured it out yet?"

He smirked. "She's learning."

"What kind of discipline are we talking about here? Curfews? Time-outs? That kind of stuff?"

"Little beyond that."

"How did Wanda react?"

"The slut went off to cavort with the Devil. And Angela wasn't far behind."

The skin on my face went tight as the friendliness flaked right off.

"Use your belt, or just your hands?"

Jonas read my eyes and scooched his chair back a few inches.

"Whoa," he said. "I just did what any father would do raising up two wild ones. Nothing wrong with that."

"Did you get that from the Good Book too?"

He jumped to his feet.

"I'm a good father. And don't need to take this from you."

Memories of Dominic danced in my head. But at least he hadn't used God's word as an excuse.

"You son of a bitch."

"No reason to talk to me like that. I did right."

"Angela is dead. And who in hell knows where Wanda is. And you honestly believe you did *right*?"

Jonas headed for the door "I'm out of here," he said. "Can't blame me for what happened."

I let him go. Another minute and I'd have taken him apart.

I walked out to the street and waited for Luce.

Overhead, purple-bellied clouds fringed with gray the color of smoke drifted like an armada of ghost ships.

A few minutes later she joined me.

"How did it go with Adele?" I asked.

"I got an earful. Old Jonas is quite the taskmaster. She said it wasn't his fault. The kids needed it. And she needed it too."

"All-American family," I said.

"Pollutants is more like it. And she's as bad as he is. She enabled him. Probably encouraged him to whack the kids around so he'd lay off her."

"They deserve each other."

"That they do."

"People like that need to have their pilot light put out."

"Not your job, Jackson. Remember, you're a consultant."

"You ought to try it sometime," I said. "It's actually quite freeing."

"I notice," she said.

"I need another favor."

"I'm about fresh out, Jackson."

"Run Wanda Klemper through the system."

"Why not," she said with a sigh.

In the *Inferno,* Dante said that each of hell's flames was a sinner. If he was right, Jonas and Adele would soon help light the lower reaches of hell.

But the image was small comfort.

They'd driven one daughter into the streets and the

other to a fiery death in a Hell's Kitchen warehouse. No charges would ever be brought. There would be no final reckoning. At least not in this world. And Jonas and Adele would spend the rest of their truly twisted lives playing the grieving parents to anyone who would listen.

15

Allie sculpted geometric shapes in the orzo with her fork, DeeDee's attention was hovering somewhere in the ether, and my snappy repartee was greeted with sublime indifference.

The dinner was supposed to be a celebration, but it had all the trappings of a wake.

Allie and I had been together for a year. To mark the occasion, I'd made reservations at Bird, a trendy SoHo bistro where the lights were dim, the portions fit for gnomes, and the waitstaff annoyingly cheerful. I'd neglected the ladies in my life and expected some time in the penalty box. But this was purgatory.

I threw my napkin on the table.

"What's going on?"

Allie set the fork down and looked at me. "I have a new boss," she said.

"But you run the creative department. Hell, you were their first hire when they started the agency."

"Business stinks, Steeg. The economy is in a sludge pit and client budgets are cut to the bone."

"Doesn't sound like a creative problem."

"It's not. But the imbeciles who run my crazy house think that change has a revivifying power. So they create a new title. Creative executive. Catchy, huh?"

"Who's the lucky man . . . or woman?"

"Remember the guy who had his caricature nailed to the wall at Café Buffo?"

DeeDee snapped out of her reverie. I noticed the mascara was gone.

"You mean the chinless Brit?" she said.

"Mr. Fly-Front Adult Diaper himself."

"Assholes!" DeeDee said.

"What are you going to do?" I said.

"Spoke to a headhunter. Told me to suck it up. Too many people chasing too few jobs these days. Especially at my level."

"If you decide to quit, there's always my disability pension to keep us going until you land somewhere."

She leaned over and planted a chaste peck on my lips. "A very sweet and comforting thought. But that assumes we eat every third day."

"And not too much, at that," I said.

"For now, I'll take the headhunter's advice and wait it out. If I can't write rings around that joker, I don't deserve the job."

"I'm really sorry, Allie."

"Don't be," she said. "Besides, you're right, we should be celebrating tonight. You've given me the happiest and most interesting year of my life."

I got all warm inside.

"That's the nicest thing anyone has ever said to me."

I looked at DeeDee.

"Your turn to say something really sweet about me," I said.

She brushed a hair off her forehead and pasted an approximation of a smile on her face.

"What a guy!" she said.

"That's it?"

"Not in the mood."

"What's wrong?"

"Nothing," she said.

"Then why the moping?"

She folded her arms on the table and rested her chin on top.

"Justin and I had an argument."

"Over what?"

"Nothing."

"If it were nothing, you wouldn't look suicidal."

"I haven't seen or heard from him in a week."

"Even at school?" Allie said.

"Nope," she said. "And I'm worried about him."

"Did you call him?" I said.

She nodded. "His father keeps answering."

"And what did he have to say?"

"I didn't talk to him."

"Why not?"

She threw me a look indicating rather strongly that I had just asked the dumbest question she had ever heard.

"He's his *father*!"

16

DeeDee wrinkled up her nose.

"Smells like dead fish," she said, as we took in the tired Bensonhurst neighborhood in the late-morning light.

They were the first words she'd uttered since we boarded the N train an hour before.

Our excursion to the depths of Brooklyn to see Justin had almost died aborning. First it was on. Then it was off. Then came the issue of what to wear, followed closely by the question of how Justin would react when she appeared on his doorstep. All her issues were discussed and, I thought, settled. But the "dead fish" crack told me that DeeDee was wavering again.

Most of the houses were attached two-family numbers. A couple had snowmen in front. And more than a few sported a Saint Mary on the half shell on their postage-stamp lawns.

Thanks to the Department of Sanitation snowplows, cars were buried up to their windows in hard-packed snow. Overhead, gulls floating in the crystal blue sky searched for a meal. Their prospects weren't promising.

Justin's apartment house, a dreary-looking four-story rectangle the color of soot, was the largest building on the block. An entrance alcove opened on a courtyard. In its center was an ornamental urn surrounded by a small fenced garden matted with long-dead flowers.

There was one apartment on either side of the alcove. Neither had a number. But the one on the right had a ramp.

"Justin's apartment is C2," she said. "On the right."

"How do you know?"

"The ramp. His father's paralyzed from the waist down."

"You never told me."

Her eyes suddenly flashed. "Since when do I have to tell you everything?"

I put her outburst down to hormones and let it pass.

Her hand reached for the doorbell, then dropped to her side.

"What now?" I said.

"You do it."

"Right. I forgot. His father may answer."

I rang the bell. It was one of those two-tone chimey deals.

DeeDee moved behind me.

A few long seconds later the door opened. A middle-aged man in a wheelchair eyed me suspiciously. His left eye sported a shiner.

I stepped aside, putting DeeDee front and center.

"My name's Steeg. My friend, DeeDee Santos, is here to see Justin."

She threw me a look that would have turned a gorgon to stone.

"Uh, Mr. Hapner. Justin and I are, uh, friends. From school. And I . . . haven't heard from him. I, uh, just wondered if he was all right."

Hapner's milky blue eyes shifted from DeeDee to me, lingered a bit, and lit on DeeDee again.

"He's never mentioned your name."

This was as close as I'd come to seeing her cry.

I draped my arm around DeeDee's shoulders.

I did a poor job keeping the edge from my voice. "Trust me," I said. "They're friends."

"Justin's in his room. Sleeping."

DeeDee wriggled away. "Maybe we should go, Steeg."

"I've forgotten my manners," Hapner said. "Justin doesn't have many friends stop by. Come on in."

Hapner's motorized wheelchair gave a low hum as it rolled backward down a short foyer to the living room.

DeeDee went first. I followed right behind.

The apartment was neat and simply furnished. The layout was pretty basic. Eat-in kitchen off the foyer. Two bedrooms off the living room. One door open. The other closed.

Photos of Justin sat on every flat surface. In all but the

photos of him as a young toddler he appeared detached. Posed. Staring either directly into the lens or off into the distance. There was nothing recent. And, surprisingly, no photos of Mom.

"Was Justin expecting you, DeeDee?" Hapner said.

"No. It's just that we kind of had an argument . . ."

"I'll get Justin," he said, motoring his chair toward the closed door. "Justin. You have company."

I heard a muffled, "Who?"

"Your friend DeeDee," Hapner said.

A few moments passed and then the door opened a crack. When Justin saw it was DeeDee, it opened wider.

Justin, wearing jeans and a Mets sweatshirt, stared at DeeDee with a look of confusion. "What're you doing here?" he said.

"I was worried," DeeDee said. "It's been a week since I heard from you. And . . ."

I noticed that Hapner was watching Justin closely. Justin threw him a hard stare and he looked away. His attention switched back to DeeDee.

"How did you get here?" Justin said.

"My friend Steeg brought me."

Justin's eyes settled on me. Then he turned to DeeDee.

"Let's get out of here," he said, heading for the door.

"You'll need a jacket," she said. "It's freezing."

"I'm fine," he said.

After they left, Hapner looked at me and half-shrugged.

"You know how it is at this age," he said. "Be happy when his hormones settle down."

Hapner motored over to me and held out his hand.

"Forgot my manners again," he said. "I'm Troy."

I took his hand. "I'm just Steeg."

"Odd first name."

"Family name. Never cared for my given name."

"Then Steeg it is," he said.

Each piece of upholstered furniture was tightly sealed in a plastic cocoon. Hapner and my mother, Norah, had to have had the same decorator. I settled in on the sofa. The cushion crackled under my weight.

"Can I get you something? A drink, perhaps?"

"Nothing, thanks." I pointed at the shiner. "Looks pretty nasty."

Hapner caressed it with the tip of his finger.

"It's nothing," he said, with a weak smile. "Turned around too quick and whacked myself with a doorknob."

I reached over and plucked a photo from an end table. It was a shot of five-year-old Justin staring away from the camera while sunbathing on a flat outcrop of rock on the shore of a lake.

"Good-looking kid," I said.

Troy Hapner took the photo, looked at it, and put it back.

"Yeah, he was," he said.

"Doesn't look too happy."

"Some kids hate being photographed," he said, looking at the door. "I wish he had worn his coat."

"Teenagers are indestructible," I said. "I don't see any pictures of Justin's mother."

"Since she died I keep them in albums."

"What happened?"

"Something I don't talk about. Too painful." He drummed his fingers on the arm of the chair and stared at the door. "They've been gone a long time."

"It's only been a few minutes," I said.

He looked at his watch. "Yeah, but . . ."

"Surprising that Justin doesn't have many friends stop by."

"He doesn't have many friends."

"How come?"

Hapner tapped a knee. "He spends a lot of his time looking after me. And the rest of it with his nose buried in books. IQ is off the charts."

"I guess there's a downside to genius."

"The other kids in the neighborhood see him as a bit of a nerd."

The door flew open and Justin rushed in.

"Where's DeeDee?" I said.

"Outside," he said, walking past me and into his room. The door slammed shut.

"What was that all about?" Hapner asked.

I went outside and found DeeDee crying.

"What happened?" I said.

"Take me home, Steeg."

It wasn't until the train pulled into the 14th Street station that DeeDee opened up.

"We're finished," she said.

"I'm really sorry, kiddo. His idea or yours?"

"His."

"Did he give a reason?"

"He said I didn't need him in my life."

"Did he offer specifics?"

"No."

I smiled. "Do you want me to beat him up?"

It was our private joke whenever DeeDee's world was in danger of falling apart. It usually got a laugh.

But not this time.

DeeDee said she needed a good, long cry. I took her home, tucked her into bed, and headed for Feeney's.

"Your brother was in a while ago," Nick said. "Looking for you."

"What does he need now?"

"A miracle. He just got the news. An indictment's about to come down."

17

Dawn Reposo's apartment building still looked like something floating in a petri dish. I was back for a second visit because my brother's string was running out, and because something Martine Toussaint had said was still echoing in my head.

Whores lie!

It was a truth I should have remembered.

They lie to their johns, their pimps, the police, and sometimes to their friends. Deception is their survival mechanism.

And I had the feeling Dawn was playing me. Sure, sending me to Martine could have been a tip of the hat for old times' sake. But Dawn said that she and Martine had a history. Maybe having me traipse around Martine's business was a way for Dawn to settle old scores. Or maybe it was an easy way of getting me out of her face, stopping me from asking questions she didn't want to answer.

Lots of maybes, and only one way to find out.

A haggard, portly black woman in a flowered house-dress answered Dawn's door. She looked forty, but was likely half that age. I could hear children playing in the background.

"Yeah?" she said, her eyes narrowing.

"Looking for Dawn Reposo," I said.

"Don't know who you're talking about."

"How long've you lived here?"

"Fuck is it your business?"

"Look, all I—"

"You from that clearing house that gives out million-dollar checks?"

"Nope."

"Get lost," she said, slamming the door.

I didn't have much better luck at the bodega next door. There were a couple of bikers all decked out in their colors, a burnout trying to keep warm, a Hispanic guy leafing through the porn magazines, a few women with spiked rainbow hair and so many piercings their faces looked like pincushions. It was as if I had stumbled into a rest stop for the freak parade.

I walked up to the counterman.

"Seen Rickie around lately?"

"Rickie who?"

"Rickie, the pimp," I said. "Lives upstairs."

He shook his head. "Cleared out about a week ago,"

he said. "Was real quick. One day he's here. Next day he's gone."

"What happened to his girls, Dawn and Gloria?"

"His bitches? Guess they went with him."

"You said it was real quick."

"Yeah. Couple of guys came in asking about Dawn. Told 'em where she lived."

"And?"

"Next morning Rickie came in and I mentioned that some guys were looking for Dawn. Cleared out that day."

"What'd they look like?"

"The guys? White. Didn't take a picture of 'em for my memory album."

"Rickie say where he was going?"

He made a big show of searching the counter. "Must've lost his itinerary." he said. "Look, I'm busy. Go bother someone else."

The door to Another Chance was locked. I looked in the window. It was dark.

I walked across the street to talk to my favorite doorman. He was out in traffic trying to hail a cab for a blue-haired woman swathed in fur. She was standing under the canopy looking at her watch and tapping her toe.

"Hey," I said. "How're you doing?"

"Wonderful!" he said. "The guy who almost cost me my pension."

"What're you talking about?"

"Said all I'm gonna say."

"What do I have to do with your pension?"

He waved his arm, took a deep breath, and blew his whistle.

"Cabs are like cops," he muttered. "Can't get 'em when you need 'em."

"Talk to me about your pension."

He looked at me. "You still here?"

"Did someone threaten you?"

He put his arm down and turned to face me.

"You gotta understand the situation," he said. "The wife has emphysema real bad. To boot, the sack of shit my daughter married ditched her. Now she and her two kids live with us in a one-bedroom. And I had a triple bypass a year ago."

"Sorry for your troubles."

"Thanks, but it don't pay the bills," he said. "This shit job and my pension do. And without them I'm fucked. Get the picture?"

"Tell me who threatened you, and I'll take care of it."

"You ain't got the juice."

18

The gods of fortune are a whimsical, capricious lot. When they're not playing Whac-A-Mole with your future, they're dreaming up other ways to have a good belly laugh. But every now and again, just to keep you in the game, the sadistic bastards throw you a bone.

On my way home from a thoroughly unsatisfying day of detecting, I dropped by Feeney's. To my utter delight, Ennis and Riley, the two heavies from Martine's office, were sitting at the bar.

I jerked my chin in their direction. "How long have they been here?"

"Maybe a half hour," Nick said. "Said they knew you. Wanted to know what time you usually came in."

"Really."

"Your eyes are getting all nuts. Is there a problem?"

"For them, maybe."

A couple of steelworkers in hard hats sat at the end of the bar getting an early start on the weekend. At the other end, Frank Ennis and John Riley were drinking beer straight from the bottle and doing a pretty good job of ignoring me. Two unused mugs sat on the bar between them.

I walked up to them.

"Gentlemen," I said. "I hear you're looking for me."

"Well, if it ain't the guy with one name," Riley said.

They slipped off the stools, leaned back, and each set an elbow on the bar. They were going for nonchalance but couldn't quite pull it off. Legs spread a touch too far apart. Weight evenly balanced on the balls of their feet. Ready for what whatever might come their way.

Their wait was going to be real short.

"Glad you're here, boys," I said. "Stopped by to see Martine, but the place was all locked up."

Ennis jabbed Riley in the ribs. "What'd I tell you, Johno? The guy's a pit bull. Sinks his teeth into something and don't let go." He looked at me. "So, what can we do for you?"

"This is kind of backwards. Nick says you were looking for me. But since you asked . . . Did you boys pay a visit to Dawn Reposo?"

"Don't know the name."

"Sure you do," I said. "She's an old friend of Martine's."

"You remember, Frank," Riley said. "The whore."

The muscles in my neck tightened.

"Oh yeah," Ennis said. "Skanky little thing. We did stop by. Martine wanted to set up a lunch. Kind of pick up where they left off. But she was gone."

"Any idea why?"

Riley flashed a really unctuous smirk. "Does a whore need a reason?"

Ennis's laugh sounded like the rattle of dried leaves.

I noticed that Nick was listening to this little byplay with avid interest. And from the corner of my eye I saw Kenny sitting in a back booth playing solitaire. But his Glock was on the table.

They both knew what Ennis and Riley were about to find out. It didn't matter what Dawn did for a living. She was my friend. That meant that these clowns were about to have their lights put out.

"I got a question for you, Steeg," Ennis said.

"Ask away."

"What's it gonna take for you to go away?"

"From what?"

"Stop bustin' my balls. You're a washed-up alky cop. A miserable excuse for a husband. Should I go on?"

"Please do."

"Your life is a high-wire act. Lots of derring-do, but you just keep tumbling off. And all you've got to show for it is a shitbox flop in Hell's Kitchen. Quite the résumé."

"You done sweet-talking me?"

"You gotta want something, and Martine can make it happen."

"A sit-down with some of your girls, and I'll be on my way."

Ennis shook his head. "Not gonna happen."

"What're you afraid of?"

"You're a dumb fuck," he said. "Deserve what you get."

"Beats being a pimp."

It was worth a shot just to see his reaction.

Ennis's face went dark.

Riley put a meaty hand around Ennis's biceps and tugged.

"Let's get outta here, Frank," he said. "It's not what we're here for."

"Don't go," I said. "The party's just about to get started.

Ennis shrugged his hand off.

"You don't know who you're fucking with, Steeg," he said. "Imagine your worst fear. Then dial it all the way up."

"My worst fears are crawly creatures with too many legs, and those that don't have any. If that's what you've got in mind, then I'd have to rethink things."

"You're a real funny guy."

I looked over at Kenny. The Glock was in his hand.

"Part of my charm."

"You're asking questions of people who don't want to be bothered. Poking around something that's not your business. And it stops now."

"Why is that?"

"That kid you hang out with. DeeDee?" he said with a shark grin. "Prime stuff. I could see—"

The snakes went on autopilot. And I was along for the ride.

I snatched a mug from the bar and smashed it against the bridge of Ennis's nose. Riley was so surprised he never saw the toe of my work boot crash into his crotch.

The steelworkers hoisted their shot glasses in appreciation.

When my heart finally stopped beating like a jackhammer, I took a few moments to reflect on an interesting juxtaposition of events. When I'd gone to see Martine, I hadn't pushed hard. Not hard enough that she'd have felt the need to send her apes to persuade me to back off.

And then it hit me. Terry Sloan.

As soon as I left his office, the slimy son of a bitch had to have filled her head with stories about my legendary stick-to-itiveness.

"You OK?" Nick said, stepping over Riley and Ennis.

"Never better."

"Who are these guys?"

"Couple of worms from the can I opened."

19

Martine Toussaint was becoming a distraction. Much as I enjoyed going a round with her guys, I still couldn't see any connection between her and the warehouse.

It was time to stop poking my hand in that hornet's nest and get back to my research.

I called Luce.

"Making any progress on the vics who bought it at Dave's warehouse?"

"I love the way you start a conversation," she said. "Short on social niceties. Right to business."

"Let's start over. How are you?"

"Do you really want to know?"

"Is it going to take long?"

"Probably."

"Terrific. Now, back to the vics."

"They're back-burnered. With your brother indicted, everyone's taking their time. Didn't find much anyway. Basically ordinary guys leading ordinary lives."

"Maybe. But doesn't the NYPD find the way they went out a tad disturbing?"

"That's so a couple of weeks ago," she said. "Now we're on to the next new thing. A Wall Street guy and his wife were bludgeoned to death in their East Side town house. Turns out he was major contributor to the DA's reelection campaign. The mayor's all over this one."

"Ain't life grand? Even in death guys with money get their asses kissed."

"It's what makes life so interesting."

"You mind if I kinda backtrack your former investigation?"

"Be my guest. Got some stuff be happy to share with you."

"When?"

"Not today. Up to my hips in crime."

"How's about breakfast at Feeney's tomorrow?"

"The Board of Health certifying Nick for serving what passes for food?"

"Beats me," I said.

"A rousing recommendation. By the way, I ran Wanda Klemper through the system. Couple of soliciting charges on her rap sheet. No known address."

"What a surprise," I said. "See you in the morning."

• • •

| Ching, on Tenth and Forty-fourth, was a cramped little joint with six tables and the best Peking Duck the city had to offer. Crispy skin. Moist slices of tender breast meat. And nestled in a wrap so light it had to be anchored to the table. Truth be told, I ate most of the duck while Allie contented herself with nibbling on a scallion tip dipped in hoisin sauce.

She had come straight from a client meeting and was wearing her version of a power suit: jeans and a black leather vest over a shimmering white silk turtleneck.

"How goes the great creative power-sharing experiment?" I said.

"About as expected. My new boss needs a lot of work in the 'works and plays well with others' department." With the tip of her chopsticks she snagged a stray piece of duck about the size of a postage stamp, dipped an edge in the sauce, and popped it in her mouth. "This is really good, Steeg."

"Be careful you don't fill up. I figured we'd hit Ferraro's for dessert. I was thinking tartufo."

She took a small bite of the scallion and laid it on her plate.

"Then I'd better leave room," she said.

"Let's get back to your new boss."

"Why ruin a lovely evening?"

"Because I've never seen you this miserable."

She pushed her chair back from the table a few inches, neatly folded her napkin, and placed it in her lap.

"He's cutting my tires one tread at a time."

"How so?"

"I have two associate creative directors. A copywriter and art director team. Very talented, and very loyal to me. I hired them when they were fresh out of school. Nurtured them. Promoted them. And the son of a bitch got the art director fired. And the writer's job is hanging by a thread."

"How did he manage to pull off this bit of corporate legerdemain?"

"He's very good at insidious. Undermined them with management. Sniped at their work with clients."

"And you're thinking you're not far behind."

"Just a matter of time."

"And management's going along with this?"

"All they give a damn about is revenues. The merest frown on a client's face is enough to send them into a tizzy."

"Anything I can do?"

"If you happen to run into the bastard, I pray to God you're driving." She snatched the napkin from her lap and threw it on the table. "Enough of my whining. Tell me what you've been up to."

"Still trying to clear Dave. Turning out to be Sisyphean. And the boulder's getting real heavy."

"No progress, huh?"

"Not sure. But thanks to an old friend who I believe had her own agenda, I kinda stumbled into a wasp nest."

"Some friend."

"Yeah. Anyway, it's a rehab for hookers run by an

ex-hooker with a thing for tarot cards. Could be a dead end as far as Dave's concerned, but my questions got someone real worried."

"And even if it's got nothing to do with Dave, you can't let it go."

"We're back to that asymmetrical justice business again," I said. "She's into something, and it involves some very important people."

"And?"

"Sometimes things come up that just grab on to you and don't let go. And you've got to see them through."

"Even though you could get hurt?"

I snatched the last of the duck from the plate and dipped it in the hoisin.

"You about ready to go?" I said.

"Almost. How's DeeDee?"

I told her about the episode at Justin's house.

"Puppy love's the beginning of a lifetime of anguish. How's she taking it?"

"She's a tough kid. It'll take a while, but she'll bounce back."

"We all do," she said.

"DeeDee's not the one I'm worried about."

"Justin?"

"Yep. He's got a tough road ahead of him. Father's wheelchair-bound. No friends. Hard for a kid."

"I didn't know."

"Neither did I," I said. "And there's something off about their relationship."

"How so?"

"I can't put my finger on it. But something's not kosher."

"Not your problem anymore."

"I know."

The waiter brought the check. I paid it, and we got our coats.

In the street the air vibrated with cold, and the streets appeared glazed with frozen moonlight the color of mother-of-pearl.

"Ready for the tartufo?" I said.

"Actually, I was planning on something else for dessert."

"What'd you have in mind?"

She took my arm and cuddled close. "You."

Hard to pass up.

20

Nick's cook was out of the slam and back behind the griddle. I didn't think it possible, but during his time at Rikers he had lost something off his culinary fastball. The eggs were rubbery enough to re-sole sneakers, the pancakes hard as hockey pucks, and the bacon left splinters in your gums. Attuned to the vagaries of dining at Feeney's, Luce brought her own coffee and a bag of donuts.

She looked at my plate with a peeled eye. "How do you eat this crap every day?" she said.

"It's like buying a lottery ticket. You know in your bones you're going to lose, but there's always the possibility that you're going to walk off with a steamer trunk full of dough."

"Did you ever have a meal here that gave you that feeling?"

I shook my head.

"It's what keeps me coming back."

She reached into her handbag, came out with three file folders, and passed them to me.

"Here's what we have on your vics."

I quickly went through them. One lived in New Jersey, in a town just north of the George Washington Bridge. Worked in a youth center. An uncle was listed as next of kin. Another lived in Queens with his mother. And the third, a postal employee, hailed from Bay Ridge, Brooklyn. Tutor. No next of kin. All were Caucasian, single, and in their fifties. I figured I'd start in New Jersey and work my way in, saving Brooklyn for my last stop. That way I could check in on Justin.

"Not much," I said. "Why only three?"

"Besides Martin Donnelly, all we've identified so far. The rest were pretty much carbon stains and bones. May take a little longer."

"And no one interviewed their friends and neighbors."

"I guess their dance calendars were full."

"Looks like I've got my work cut out for me."

My cell phone rang.

The conversation took less than thirty seconds.

"I've got to go," I said.

"What's up?"

"Franny, Dave's wife, is in town. Wants me to meet her."

"Everything all right?"

"Didn't sound it."

● ● ●

Franny's hotel was small and sleek, and just off Houston Street on the Lower East Side. I found her nursing a glass of white wine at the bar. The bartender stood off to the side pretending to be busy.

Franny had an off-kilter beauty and worked hard at looking good. But the lines around her mouth had deepened into a road map of life with my brother.

"Thanks for coming," she said. "I really appreciate it. Can I get you a Diet Coke or something?"

I shook my head.

Her skin had a golden hue.

"I'm good," I said. "Nice tan."

"It's what Florida's famous for. But the sun kicks the hell out of your skin."

"How are the girls?"

She took a small sip of her wine.

"They're fine," she said. "But it's a big adjustment. They miss their father. Their friends. You know the drill."

"I do."

"You still with Allie?"

"Long as she'll have me."

"I still regret that crack I made about her being Jewish. That wasn't me, Steeg."

Franny and my ex-wife, Ginny, were pretty close. And Franny harbored this fantasy of us getting back together again. The problem was that Ginny was two marriages removed from ours, and I was now spoken for. But

Franny, ever the optimist, always held out hope. And took her disappointment out on Allie.

"We all say stupid things we regret," I said. "It's over, kiddo. And all's right with the world."

"You mean it?"

Not for a minute. But sometimes you have to give family a pass.

"I do," I said. "So, what brings you back to our not so fair city?"

"Meeting with my lawyer. Got a bunch of things to work out."

"Dave know you're here?"

"No, and you're not going to tell him. That's why I picked a spot as far away from the Kitchen as I could."

If we met on the Kamchatka Peninsula, Dave would find out.

Franny lifted the glass to her lips, drained it, tapped the bar, and ordered a Johnny, water back. The bartender immediately obliged.

"Anthony called," she said. "First time in months."

"I'm surprised. You two were very close."

"I know. Dave always said he was a momma's boy."

"And now he's switched over to the dark side."

"I know my son, Steeg. He just doesn't sound like himself."

"It comes of spending too much time with his father."

"How did you avoid it?"

"Sometimes I wonder if I did."

Franny took a healthy swig of whiskey. It set off a coughing spasm that teared up her eyes.

"Maybe you should stick to wine," I said.

"Maybe I should switch to arsenic, neat," she said, settling down. "First my husband, and now my son." She held up the glass of whiskey and toasted the bar mirror. "Mother of the Year!"

"Not your fault, Franny."

"Yeah it is. I never should've had that man's children."

"You knew what he was when you married him."

She nodded. "No getting around that," she said. "Dave was like a thunderstorm. Unpredictable. Violent. But with me he was always gentle. Loving. Nothing could ever hurt me when I was with him. Romantic, huh?"

"You were young."

"But not stupid. I knew. Whoever said people are stronger in the broken places didn't know what he was talking about."

"Tell me about Anthony."

Franny's eyes were beginning to glass up. She took another sip of whiskey.

"I know my son. It's like when he was a kid and he'd done something wrong. I always knew. Could see it in his eyes. And I always managed to get it out of him. Anthony never was able to carry a secret for long. But he's different now. He's carrying a heavy load, Steeg. And I can't get it out of him with a pry bar."

"He's not a kid anymore, Franny."

"And therein lies the problem."

"What do you want me to do?"

"Talk to him. See if you can make any sense of it."

"He won't talk to me. I tried."

She pushed the whiskey away.

"What am I going to do? My son is turning into his father."

"So you're really going through with the divorce."

She shook her head. "If I did, who would protect my son?"

21

The next morning I rented a car with a GPS system and headed for the leafy—at least in summer— suburb of Danners Ferry, New Jersey.

The inventor of GPS should be honored with a national holiday. You punch in an address—and voilà!—even the most directionally challenged can find their way to any spot on the globe. I crossed the George Washington Bridge, took a scenic trip north on the Palisades Parkway, and made it in under an hour.

Danners Ferry was pretty much what I'd expected. Tidy homes. Snow-covered lawns. Freshly plowed streets. A terrific view of the Hudson. And sidewalks completely devoid of people.

According to the file Luce had given me, Charles Bingham, vic number one on my list, had lived alone. To get a sense of the late Mr. Bingham—put him into some kind of context—I decided to check out his house. I pulled into a spot in front of 110 Oak Street and parked behind a late-model Honda. The house was your basic Cape Cod with white siding and peeling black paint on the shutters. I walked up to the door, but it swung open before I had a chance to ring the bell.

A pretty teenaged girl with spiked hair and studs running up and down her left ear stood in the doorway. She had twin boys in tow. They were all dressed for the coming Ice Age.

She appeared startled.

That made two of us.

"Is this Charles Bingham's house?"

"Duh! This is *110* Oak," she said, revealing a tongue stud as big as a marble. It was a wonder she could form words. "The creepazoid lives at 109, across the street."

I looked across the street.

"The white Colonial with the U-Haul truck parked in the driveway?" I said.

"That's the one."

"Why'd you call him a creepazoid?"

"Because he's a *freak*!"

"That clears it up. Define *freak*."

She shrugged as if losing patience with giving self-evident answers to my pointless questions.

"I don't know," she said. "He just is."

I took another shot.

"Could you try being a touch more specific?"

"He's weird, that's all. Got this train set that takes up the whole living room. Invites all the neighborhood kids to play with it on Christmas. On Easter he dresses up in a pink bunny suit and buries eggs all over the property. Everyone thinks it's a hoot."

"Seems like a good neighbor."

"Maybe. I don't know. I just don't like the way he looks at the kids. Creeps me out."

"Anyone in the neighborhood he's close to?"

"*Puhleeze?* Look, I've got to get these two little rug rats to their playdates. If I'm even a minute late I'm gonna be fired."

She grabbed the kids by the hand and dragged them to the Honda.

I crossed the street, climbed the stairway to the porch, and rang the bell. A white-haired woman opened the door.

"Can I help you?" she said.

"Is this the home of Charles Bingham?"

She looked at me as if waiting for another shoe to drop.

I handed her my card. "I'm investigating his murder. And I wonder—"

Her gaze had drifted to my card, but then came back to me.

"You from the insurance company?"

"No."

She made a face and handed my card back.

"You'll have to speak to my husband. Wait here."

She closed the door.

A few minutes later a white-haired gent, with a scowl on his face and a stomach that slopped over his jeans, opened the door.

"What's this about?" he said.

"Are you related to Charles Bingham?"

"I'm Sam Bingham, Charlie's uncle. And you are?"

I skipped the card routine.

"Name's Steeg. And I'm sorry for your loss. Do you have a few minutes?"

"You're not from the insurance company? They said someone would come by."

"Afraid not."

"Then what do we have to talk about?"

"Well, maybe I can help make the insurance thing happen."

"Come back when you have the check," he said, slamming the door in my face.

Bereavement takes many forms.

I went back to the car and punched in the address of the Danners Ferry Youth Center, Bingham's last place of employment.

Fifteen minutes later, I pulled into the parking lot.

The lobby was a jumble of activity. Phone ringing off the hook. Hyperactive kids. Somewhere out of sight a pool pumped out enough noxious fumes to stun a herd of wildebeests. And the reception counter was four deep with people who had problems that needed immediate fixing. Three harried-looking women stood behind the counter doing their best to handle the load. I didn't envy them.

I got in line and waited my turn. It took a while, but I finally made it to the counter.

A pretty woman with tired eyes hung up the phone and gave me what passed for her full attention. Her name tag said "Deb."

She flashed me a warm smile. I had the feeling she really meant it.

"How can I help you?" she said.

"Is it always like this?"

"Pretty much. Kind of frantic, isn't it?"

"Like a Chinese fire drill."

Her smile widened.

"So, what can I do for you?"

"Who can I talk to about Charles Bingham?"

Her smile faded.

"It's so sad," she said.

"Yeah. Good guy?"

The telephone rang and Deb reached for it. She seemed relieved. After a few seconds of conversation she transferred the call and turned her attention back to me.

"I think you ought to speak to our director, Ralph Patterson," she said. "Your name?"

I told her.

She picked up the phone and punched in a number.

"Ralph, someone is here asking about Charlie." She paused. "Fine. I'll bring him up."

She turned back to me.

"I'll take you to his office."

Deb came out from behind the counter. I followed her up two flights of stairs and down a long corridor to an open door. A very large black man stood in the doorway with his arms folded across his chest.

"Here we are, Mr. Steeg," she said. "Ralph should be able to answer all your questions."

"Thanks, Deb," Patterson said.

He had a short-cropped beard, a tiny diamond in his left earlobe, and a decidedly unfriendly expression on his face.

I held out my hand. His arms remained crossed over his chest.

This was going well.

"You're here about Charlie Bingham," Patterson said.

"Just need a few minutes of your time," I said, handing him my card.

He glanced at it, and slipped it into his shirt pocket.

The office behind him was small and crowded with sports trophies.

Patterson didn't invite me in.

"All I can tell you is that Charlie worked here up to a few months ago," he said.

"When did he start?"

"Couple of years ago."

"And his job?"

"A little of this, and a little of that."

"You're not exactly being forthcoming here," I said.

"Telling you all I can tell you."

"Bingham quit?"

"We had a difference of opinion."

"Over what?"

"That's confidential."

"Why?"

"'Cause I said so. What's your interest in Charlie?"

"He died in a fire along with five other men. They were stashed in packing crates in the basement of a warehouse. And sexually mutilated. Bingham was probably alive when the fire took him. For reasons known only to them, the NYPD is losing interest in the case. I'm not."

Patterson's face never changed expression. Even the mutilation part failed to move him.

He took my card out of his pocket and looked at it again.

"You're not a cop," he said.

"Was. I'm doing this on my own nickel."

"Hell of a way for Charlie to go. But I can't help you."

"Why not?"

"What do you think of our facility?"

"Looks like you're doing the Lord's work."

"And that's exactly what we're going to keep on doing. You have a good day, sir."

My next stop was Queens.

• • •

Beginning at the Queensborough Bridge and ending over seven miles later in the bowels of the borough, Queens Boulevard is a particularly daunting stretch of twelve-lane thoroughfare. And the late Augie Frena had lived smack dab in its center. Without my trusty GPS, I would have wound up in Nebraska.

Frena's apartment house was a looming monster of a building that probably held enough tenants to stock a reasonably sized small town. It took half an hour to find a parking spot.

The lobby was long on mailboxes. Short on amenities.

I hopped an elevator and rode it to the fifteenth floor. Metal doors lined the corridor. Gray floor covering. The smell of disinfectant in the air. It brought Sing Sing to mind.

I rang the bell of apartment 15C.

There was the sound of shoes scuffing against a hardwood floor.

A few seconds later, a dark and watery eye appeared at the peephole.

"What do you want?" it said.

"Mrs. Frena? I'd like to talk to you about Augie."

"He was a good boy. Get lost!"

The eye disappeared, and I heard it shuffle off.

And that ended my second interview of the day.

But I was in the mood to poke around a bit.

The lobby of the building was empty, and the glacial cold dissuaded any neighbors from shooting the breeze out front. Figuring that Frena needed a carton of milk every now and then, I stopped in at a convenience store down the block. It was empty. A glum-looking Hispanic guy manned the counter. To get him in the right frame of mind, I bought a Diet Coke and a bag of chips. The perfect lunch for a man on the go.

"Shitty weather," I said.

He glanced outside at a cold, flat day. "Tell me about it," he said. "Took in just about enough cash today to buy a rope to hang myself."

I ripped open the bag of chips and dove in.

"Augie Frena ever stop in here? Lives in the building up the block?"

He looked up at the ceiling, as if the mystery of the name was somehow nestled in the light fixtures.

"Augie Frena. Augie Frena," he repeated.

"Lives with his mother?" I prompted.

"Oh, that Augie Frena," he said, as if Queens was crawling with Augie Frenas. "The fucked-up guy who lives with the *bruja,* the witch."

"Sounds like her."

"That old broad is some piece of work. Don't know how he does it. Yeah, he comes in every morning. Same routine. Checks out the *Enquirer.* Picks up the *Post,* gets two coffees, and stuffs his pockets with sugar packets. Guy has a hell of a sweet tooth. Haven't seen him around lately, though."

"What can you tell me about him?"

His eyes narrowed. "Why do you wanna know?"

I plucked a Milky Way off a shelf and laid it on the counter along with a twenty.

"That about cover it?" I said.

He pocketed the twenty.

"He's a fucking grown man living with his mother. What more do you need to know?"

"Did you two ever talk?"

"About what?"

"Anything. His job. Girlfriends. Why the Yankees suck this year. You know. Stuff."

"Never mentioned a job. Smelled like a sewer. Dressed like a bag lady. Who the fuck would hire him? And girlfriends? Gimme a break!"

"Why do you say that?"

"He was kind of off."

"Define *off*."

"Like not normal, for a guy."

"Can you narrow that down?"

An elderly couple entered the store and walked up to the counter.

The counterman shook his head in a way that said this conversation was over. "I got a business to run. Want another Milky Way? On the house."

I passed.

It was getting late, and I figured I'd save Brooklyn for another time. But the day wasn't a total loss. Bingham and Frena fit a profile: loners who by reason of preference, or glitches in their internal wiring, lived out their lives in the dark places where the secrets are stored. Cady fit the profile too. Donnelly had been married. But from what his wife had told me, it wasn't a stretch to include him.

I was beginning to get a pretty good idea of what those secrets were. That got me to thinking that Martine was a sidetrack, and my original theory needed a major overhaul.

22

returned the car to the rental company, bid the GPS a fond and heartfelt good-bye, and walked back to my apartment.

A black Mercedes sat out front.

Dave, all bundled up in a black cashmere overcoat, sat in the backseat. Anthony sat next to him. Tommy Cisco was behind the wheel. Dave lowered the window and motioned for me to join him.

A special ending to a special day.

"Cisco, take a hike," Dave said. "Anthony, let your uncle sit next to me. Get in the front."

Cisco got out, lit up a smoke, and stationed himself next to the hood. Anthony moved into Cisco's spot, and when the musical chairs was done, I slid in beside my brother.

An old homeless guy, a black man with skin the color of deeply tanned leather, moved slowly past our car. He walked with a pronounced limp and used a broken table leg for support. At his feet he had four bulging suitcases lashed with rope. He lifted one, limped a few feet, set it down, and returned for another, which he placed next to the first suitcase. When they were all together, he repeated the process.

He had our attention.

As he passed, Cisco flicked his cigarette in his direction. It exploded against the suitcase in a shower of sparks. With a smirk on his face, Cisco fist-pumped a triumphant *Yes!*

Tommy Cisco and I were about to go for round two. I opened the door, but Dave pulled me back.

"All in good time," he said. "Right now I've got more important things to get out of the way."

"Like what?"

"I've got this problem, Jake," Dave said.

"Besides the indictment?"

"I've been kicking around the question of who I can trust."

"And where do you come out?"

"You met with Franny."

"You know that, how?"

"I know everything that happens in this city."

"She had a drink. I didn't. We talked."

"You didn't tell me."

"She asked me not to."

"Not surprised. But it doesn't wash."

"That I gave Franny my word?"

Dave's stump stroked the pebbled surface of his cheek.

He was pissed, and I didn't give a damn.

"That sometimes you have a problem differentiating between blood and an outsider," he said.

"Anthony," I said. "Your father and I need some privacy."

Anthony swung his door open. Dave stopped him.

"Stay right where you are, kid," Dave said. "I want you to hear this."

"Don't do this, Dave."

"It's gonna be OK. Consider it part of my son's continuing education. Now, where were we?"

"Something about Franny being an outsider. And here I am thinking she's your wife."

"But not blood."

Anthony's hands gripped the steering wheel so tightly his knuckles were white.

"She's the mother of your children."

"But not my blood," he said.

"You really need to see a shrink."

"This isn't about me, Jake. It's about who I can and can't trust. You're the one in the spotlight."

I grabbed the door handle.

"See ya," I said.

He reached over, and his hand clamped down on mine and held it.

"What'd you two talk about?" he said.

"Cabbages and kings."

His smile was cold.

"You never change, do you?"

"What you see is what you get. But you know that."

"She gonna go through with it?"

"The divorce?"

"Yeah."

"I'll tell you this much, Dave. You're not number one on her People I Worry About list. Anthony occupies the top spot now."

Anthony's hands began to tremble.

"My son is *my* problem."

"No, Anthony's your joint problem. Whatever he's doing for you goes against who he is. And when he blows, you're not gonna be happy with the results."

Dave released his grip on my hand.

"Don't you think you're being a bit dramatic here?"

"If you're looking for a reason why your marriage is in the dumper, you found it."

"Anything else, Dr. Laura?"

I opened the door.

"I'm done," I said.

"Not quite yet. Like I said, nothing escapes my attention."

"You're being cryptic again."

"Then let's try direct. I hear you've made some people very angry."

"That's what your pet councilman Terry said."

My brother seemed surprised.

"You talked to him?" he said.

"In the interests of saving your sorry ass. But your old buddy wasn't very helpful."

"What did he say?"

"He'd rather throw you under the bus than the people I've pissed off."

"Fucking Terry," he mumbled. "His time'll come."

"Can you put any names to these people?"

He shook his head.

"Then I guess I'll have to," I said.

"You're dealing with a different kind of *dangerous* than you're used to, Jake."

"In what way?"

"They're public figures. Men with reputations to protect. And with you poking around in their business and threatening to expose their dirty little secrets, they'll get desperate."

"Tough shit."

"You still don't get it. To keep out of the newspapers they'll come at you in ways you didn't think possible."

"Then I'll have to deal with it. Some kid in Bed-Stuy gets busted for dealing a little weed and he goes straight to the slam. These jokers are up to far worse and expect to skate. Screw 'em!"

Dave flashed me a crooked grin. "And I'm supposed to be the hardhead."

I left Dave and Anthony and went up to my apartment. It was as cold and dark as a cave. Figuring that a little sunlight wouldn't hurt, I walked over to the living room window and drew open the blinds.

23

n less than ten minutes hordes of black-uniformed, body-armored SWAT types had arrived at my apartment, strung yards of yellow tape, and declared it a crime scene.

Lieutenant Finbar Reagan, a hulking, but surprisingly agile Irishman with whom I had had a nodding acquaintance, ran the show.

"So let me get this straight, Steeg," he said. "You walk into your apartment, go straight to the window, and pow!"

"Not quite. I walked over to the window, opened the blinds, and *then* pow! Slug crashed through the window, and I hit the deck."

"If I were you, I'd set up a shrine to your landlord."

"Why's that?"

"Had the foresight to install a window gate. Deflected

the bullet. Slug wound up in your wall. One of my guys is digging it out."

A uniform walked up to Reagan.

"Check this out, Finn," he said. "We were on our way to the roof of the building across the street when we heard some yelling coming from a fourth-floor apartment. We go in and find this elderly couple tied up in the bedroom. She's gagged, but her husband managed to work his gag loose and is shouting to beat the band."

"Has to be the Gargiullos," I said. "Vito and Amelia. He's in his eighties. Guy was a baker. Arms as big around as my thighs. They okay?"

"Think so. Paramedics are looking at them. Anyway, they're bringing groceries in and two guys do a push-in. Tie the old folks up. Tell 'em they're not gonna hurt 'em, and stash 'em in the bedroom. Hang around for three, four hours, and then split."

Reagan moved to the window.

"Show me the apartment," he said.

"Right across the way," I said. "On the same floor as mine."

"That explains the hole in your wall."

He walked over to the tech digging out the slug.

I trailed right behind.

"Got it yet?" Reagan said.

"Just about."

The tech pulled a tool that looked like a forceps out of his bag, stuck it in the hole, came out with the round, and dropped it in the palm of Reagan's outstretched hand.

"Shit!" Reagan said. "I've seen this little beauty before."

"You can identify it?"

"It's deformed, but I think so. Brings me back to my youth."

"How so?"

"This little guy is a NATO sniper round. State of the art. The shooter probably used a scope."

"I'm impressed, Finn. I really am. I can't tell the difference between a BB and a brick. How come you know this stuff?"

"Six years as a Marine sniper," he said. "Any idea why anyone would go to this trouble and expense to punch your ticket?"

"Not a clue."

"Steeg, what's going on? Why're all these cops dressed like Space Troopers here?"

DeeDee stood in the doorway with her arms wrapped tightly around her body.

"I guess I really annoyed someone, kiddo."

"The cop downstairs said there was a shooting a couple of floors up," she said. "So I run upstairs, and it's you."

I walked over and put my arm around her shoulders. She was trembling.

"Yeah, but as you can plainly see, he missed. Nothing to worry about."

She put her fingers on my cheek.

"Really? Then why is blood streaming down your face?"

I pulled a handkerchief out of my pocket and swiped it across my cheek. It came back red.

"Came through the window," I said. "Must have been some flying glass."

"Other than that you're good, right?"

"As gold."

She turned to Reagan.

"And what the hell are you fat asses doing about it?" she said, her voice rising. "You've got cops all over the building knocking on doors, when it's obvious even to a kid like me that the guy who did this is still out there. Fucking *unbelievable*! You people couldn't catch rain with a bucket!"

Reagan looked down at DeeDee as if he were regarding a pesky Lilliputian.

"You've got some mouth on you, little girl," he said.

"That seems to be the consensus," I agreed, hugging DeeDee tighter.

"But the kid's right. The guy's still out there, Steeg."

"He had a scope," I said. "It could have been a warning."

Reagan shrugged. "Could be. Sure you want to chance it?"

"Can you think of an alternative?"

"Yeah. Stop holding out on me."

After Reagan left, I went into the bathroom to get a Band-Aid. The cut on my cheek was small but deep. I rinsed it with cold water. Dried it. And stuck the Band-Aid on. When I came out, DeeDee was sitting on the sofa crying.

I sat down next to her, slung my arm over her shoulder, and pulled her close.

"It's over. I'm fine. So why're you crying?"

"All this time, I've taken you for granted."

"What's that supposed to mean?"

"You're the reason I'm me. The thought of anything happening to you is just . . ."

"Let's get out of here," I said.

24

Armand Federov was the last vic on my list.

By all accounts, he was the reincarnation of Mother Teresa. Caring neighbor. Dedicated teacher. Parents and students loved him. Spent his spare time tutoring shelter kids, and never asked for a penny. Took them to ball games. Slipped their families money when they were short. Served Thanksgiving meals to the homeless at a local Lutheran church. The pastor was Federov's biggest fan of all. Claimed Federov did God's work, and the world was worse off for his loss.

On the debit side of the ledger, Federov, like the others, was a fringe guy. No friends. No romantic entanglements. Just his work to keep him warm on cold winter nights.

But he didn't quite fit the profile.

Truth be told, I would have been surprised if he had. I learned long ago that most investigations don't fit into neat little boxes. But if you kept at them long enough, chances were all would be revealed. That belief was the only thing cops had to hold on to. And it kept the good ones from eating their guns.

By the time I was done with Federov, it was only noon. My rental car had a GPS, and I was in the Bay Ridge section of Brooklyn. An extraordinary confluence of events that brought Justin Hapner to mind. And Bensonhurst was close by.

I spotted a parking spot that some guy had spent hours digging his car out of. Better yet, it was right across the street from Justin's apartment house.

I got out of the car and my cell phone rang.

"Steeg, it's Luce. Where are you?"

I told her.

"What's up?" I said.

"There's been another one. Just came over the wire."

I parked in the shadow of the Wonder Wheel, on Surf and West Twelfth, and walked a short block to the crime scene. Overhead, serious-looking clouds were blowing in off the Atlantic, turning it white with chop.

Detective Esteban "Cholo" Somoza stood just outside the yellow tape, directing the action. A few joggers, a sprinkling of truants, and a clutch of red-cheeked babushkas and their equally red-cheeked men stood on the boardwalk watching him do his thing.

Cholo was a big man who favored black ink tattoos,

custom choppers, and people who didn't bullshit him. We'd always got along just fine.

"Hey, Cholo. How goes it?"

"Look what the tide washed up," he said. "What in hell are you doing here, Steeg?"

"Luce said you might have something I want to see."

"She's one of the good guys. Always liked her. Follow me, and be careful where you walk. The techs are just about finished, but . . ."

"I know the drill. It's still your crime scene."

"My own little piece of hell," he said. "I hear you're off the sauce."

I nodded. "Used to be my little piece of hell."

"Was it tough?"

"Like pulling a glass-studded rope through my brain."

Cholo put his arm on my shoulder and kept his voice low.

"I had the same deal with blow," he said. "I'm clean now, but a day doesn't go by that I don't miss it."

"The junkie's lament. Ain't an addictive personality grand?"

"A bitch, ain't it? Fuck it! Let's go see a stiff."

I followed Cholo a few yards under the boardwalk to to where the victim—or what was left of him—was lying on his back. I couldn't count the puncture wounds that covered his body. And the slashes that crisscrossed his face looked like someone had used it for a demented game of tic-tac-toe. The snow between his legs was dyed vermillion.

"There he is in living color," Cholo said.

"Holy shit!" I said.

"Tell me about it. Makes the Top Ten list of the worst I ever saw. When I first laid eyes on him I nearly puked."

"Eminently understandable."

"You know the first thing that jumped into my mind?"

"Better him than you?"

"OK, the second thing. Remember that poem about Lizzie Borden? Took an axe and gave her mother forty whacks?"

"And when she saw what she had done, she gave her father forty-one."

"Yeah. Only whoever turned this guy into tatters used a knife as sharp as a scalpel. And check the crotch. Lot of anger here, Steeg."

I noticed there was no blood spatter, and mentioned it to Cholo.

"Good eye," he said. "We found a shitload of blood at the bottom of the stairs, and drag marks leading here."

"Footprints?"

He shook his head.

"The doer cleaned up after himself. We also ruled out robbery. Guy had over five hundred in his wallet."

"Who found him?"

"A bum." Cholo pointed at a large carton deep under the boardwalk, about twenty yards away. "Lives over there. Spent the night scavenging. Found him when he got home. Flagged down a patrol car. And here we are."

"So he saw and heard nothing."

"Absolutely nada."

Cholo jerked his chin at the body. "Word is you have an interest in these guys."

"Where'd you hear that?"

"One Police Plaza is a regular yenta fest."

"I do."

"Any help would be appreciated."

I clapped Cholo on the shoulder.

"If I manage to stumble across something in my wanderings, you'll be the first person I call," I said. "Count on it."

"Sure you will," he snickered.

"So tell me, when did you become so callous, Cholo, my friend?"

"Comes of years cleaning up after psychos."

I turned to leave, but Cholo's voice stopped me.

"By the way, we found sticks topped with cotton candy and arranged like a bouquet of flowers next to the body. Nice touch, huh?"

"Very creative. It seems like the guy was going for romance."

"Sometimes being a romantic has its downside," Cholo said. "Guy brings his true love a cotton candy bouquet. She was expecting diamonds. It pisses her off, and he winds up being reduced to a mess of Kibbles."

"Love is a bitch."

25

A lot of anger here.

That had to be the understatement of the eon. Six packing crates. Six men. And then there was the fire. The ME's report said that a couple of the men were alive when the fire started. Why bring them to the warehouse? That one was easy. For the same reason Angela and the guys she was with picked it for a Christmas Eve party. It was abandoned, therefore private. But why would the killer torch the place and destroy his perfect hidey-hole?

And that left the latest victims. The guy in a West Side hotel. Walter Cady, the Bowery flop manager. The man in Coney Island. And who knows how many others waiting to be discovered. The murders were getting closer in time, and the killer's rage was increasing. Once the warehouse was gone, the killer was out of his comfort zone. And more prone to mistakes. And that meant nailing the son of a bitch was just a matter of time.

It was speculation. But there was logic to it, and it felt right. But there was one more issue that needed to be resolved.

I called Luce.

"Thanks for the heads-up," I said. "And Cholo sends his regards."

"Could be the last heads-up you'll get from me."

"Meaning?"

"My boss told me I may be facing a departmental trial."

"For what?"

"Conduct unbecoming. Lifestyle issues, he said. Translation . . . being gay."

Dave's warning rumbled in my head. *They'll come at you in ways you didn't think possible.*

"And the specifics?"

"Internal Affairs is poking around my life and trying to come up with some."

"I'm sorry I got you into this, kiddo. I'm the one they should've dropped the hammer on."

"If you can't help a friend . . ."

"Somehow I'll make this right."

"That's real sweet, but screw *right*! I want to see all those fat cat bastards go down. So, what can I do for you?"

"Got a new theory."

"Lay it on me."

"The doer's gender may be wrong."

"We've been through this already and rejected it."

"I know. But we didn't take the killer's occupation into account. Think gay and on the stroll."

"A gay hustler?"

"Yeah," I said. "So far none of the vics—even the married guy—seem to be into women. Given the sexual nature of the crime, a male prostitute fits the bill."

A few seconds passed while Luce considered this new wrinkle.

"Plausible," she said. "Even when you throw in the Rohypnol."

"Exactly what I was thinking. Everything remains the same, except gender."

"It does," she said. "And wouldn't hurt to check it out. Let me reach out to my connections in the community. I'll get back to you."

I dropped the phone in my pocket, looked up, and saw Kenny Apple walking up to me.

"I've got to hand it to you, Steeg. When you take a road trip, you manage to hit all the high spots," he said.

"What are you talking about?"

"There's nothing to be said for Coney Island this time of year. Or most other times, either. Cold. Dreary. And bloody."

"You followed me? What the hell for?"

"Heard about the shooting. Figured you could use some backup."

I loved Kenny Apple.

"See anything interesting?"

"In a manner of speaking."

"Like what?"

"Spotted him right away. When you left your apartment. Big guy with close-cropped hair. Driving an old, gray Ford. Trying to blend in, I guess. Was with you every step of the way. When you dropped the car off, he took off."

"That sounds like Riley. I don't suppose you followed him?"

"Tried to, but lost him in rush-hour traffic."

"Terrific."

"Look, I do two things really well. Make numbers sing and shoot people. And that's about it. But not to worry, he'll be back again."

"This is turning into a fine kettle of fish, isn't it?"

"Certainly is."

I looked at my watch.

"Haven't eaten all day. Want to grab a bite?"

"I'm going to take a nap. Promise me you'll stay pretty much close to home for the next day or so."

"Consider it a solemn oath."

I walked the few blocks to Feeney's, looked through the window, saw the usual suspects eating the usual slop, and lost my appetite.

The night was still young. And Ennis and Riley were somewhere out there.

And that rankled.

But not for long.

I headed back to my apartment. A gray Ford was parked at the pump, right out front.

The snakes in my head snapped awake.

Riley was behind the wheel. Ennis sat in the passenger seat. His eyes were black, and his nose was heavily bandaged. The mystery lady sat in back.

I walked over.

Martine rolled the window down. She had a deck of tarot cards in her hand.

"What am I going to do with you, Steeg?" she said.

"The bullet through my window says you pretty much made up your mind."

"If I had, we wouldn't be having this conversation."

"Lucky me."

"I could make you rich, Steeg."

"Maybe. But then I wouldn't have anything to bitch about."

"Final offer."

"Dawn said you two had a history."

Her lips curled into a smile.

"Whores don't have a history. No future, either. Only a now."

"What happened to her?"

"Could be anywhere," she said. "Or nowhere. Who knows what's in a whore's mind?"

"What's in yours, Martine?"

"Touché."

Her fingers worked the cards. Fanning them out, then

squaring them. Over and over. Making sure the edges were perfectly straight.

"You ever been to Haiti?" she said.

"Nope."

"Makes the rest of the shitbox countries in the world look like luxury resorts."

"*Poor* don't get you a Get Out of Jail Free card. And selling the services of women you're supposed to be helping isn't going to earn you a spot in heaven."

Her face tightened. "I worked hard to get to this place. And I won't let you ruin it."

"You're not the first who's ever said that."

"But I'll be the last." Her face contorted into a tight, ugly mask. "I'm not going back, Steeg."

"What do the cards have to say about that?"

She fanned them one more time and held them out.

"Let's see," she said. "Pick one."

I plucked a card from the center.

Riley started the car up and shifted it into gear.

"No more warnings, Steeg," she said.

When they pulled away, I turned the card over and looked at it.

It was a skeleton riding a pale white horse.

Just a bit of sleight of hand on Martine's part, I was sure. Well, almost sure.

26

Me and John Walker parted ways a long time ago. Long enough that by now, the days are OK. But the nights are still a bit problematic. Some are worse than others. And a few make it to Category Five.

It starts with an icicle working its way into the base of my brain. Then it's an electric slide to tremors, nausea, and sweat so cold the heat of a thousand suns wouldn't even begin to warm me.

Thanks to Martine, this was one of those nights.

So I did what I usually do when a meltdown is roaring in on a bullet train. Scooted over to see Allie. For some reason Johnny moved on to easier pickings when I was with her.

She reached up and cradled my face in her hand.

"You sounded terrible on the phone," she said. "And you look worse. What's wrong?"

"Remember the evil monkeys from *The Wizard of Oz*? Well, they've taken over my bedroom. I closed my eyes and clicked my red slippers, but . . ."

"When you opened them you weren't back home in Kansas."

"I am now."

She took my hand and led me to the sofa, drew me down beside her, and put my head on her lap. Her hand felt warm on my skin.

"Want to talk about it?" Allie said.

"And ruin a perfectly good rest of the evening? Let's talk about happy things. Like your job."

"I'm off suicide watch. My new boss is now my fired boss."

"Get out!"

"Happened in the twinkle of an eye. Something about a YouTube video."

"And the subject matter?"

"A Roman orgy kind of thing complete with togas and drugs."

"And your fired boss was the leading sybarite?"

"Caligula, actually. The link was sent to agency management, and clients."

"Was the sender anyone we know?"

"Hand to God it wasn't me, but it could've been anyone. His enemies were legion. When security escorted him out the door, a collective cheer went up on Madison Avenue."

"So, all's well that ends well."

"Very well," she said. "Enough about me. How's DeeDee doing?"

"What's that they say about first loves?"

"You never forget them," Allie said.

"Do you remember your first love?"

"Herbie Aronson. He was twelve. I was ten. Lived in my apartment house in Canarsie. Sixth floor. I lived on the fifth. I could see his apartment across the courtyard. I remember sitting at my living room window for hours just waiting for him to appear at his window. When he did I would melt. Of course, he would have nothing to do with me."

"What made you so smitten?"

"His clear complexion."

"Sounds serious."

"Oh, it was. I even became friendly with his sister, a despicable little trollop, just to get close to him."

"Did it work?"

"Do things ever work when you're ten and in love?"

"I guess not."

"Herbie would tickle the ivories for hours on end. How they ever managed to schlep a piano up five flights of stairs and wedge it into that tiny apartment was always a mystery. But somehow they did, and Herbie would bang away until the neighbors complained. I thought it was glorious."

"I take it Herbie wasn't the athletic type."

"Sports were for goons. Herbie was *sensitive*. In fact, I spent a lot of time imagining our life together. We'd have our own apartment in our parents' apartment house. Herbie would be a concert pianist, and I would be his bookish but clever impresario. Arranging concert dates. Handling interviews with the press. Writing his biography. That sort of stuff."

"All this when you were ten. Who'd have thought?"

"I was a very precocious child."

"Whatever happened to Herbie?"

"Dropped out of Brooklyn College, dealt weed for a time, and wound up selling vacuum cleaners door-to-door."

"Ah. The promise of youth dashed against the jagged rocks of life."

"Who was your first love, Steeg?"

"You."

I could feel the smile in her touch.

"Sometimes it's good to be lied to," she said. "It's been a long day.

"For both of us," I agreed.

"What do you have in mind?"

"I thought you'd never ask."

27

The next morning Allie was up and out of the house before I awoke. There was a note lying on top of my clothes. *Plenty of stuff in the fridge for breakfast,* it said. I checked. A package of baby carrots. A couple of limp asparagus spears. A plastic baggy chockfull of bean sprouts. And a brick of soy.

Visions of Feeney's danced in my head.

When I arrived, Nick was behind the bar engaged in one of his favorite pastimes. Adulterating the inventory.

"Still pouring the cheap stuff into the top-shelf bottles?" I said.

"The barflies can't tell the difference anyway. Drink antifreeze if the label was pretty."

"What else is going on?"

"Your brother."

"What's he up to now?"

"Does going nuts count?"

"Not a new condition."

"This is. He trusts no one. Hammering all of us, especially Anthony. Riding the kid into the ground."

"Why?"

"Ask the crazy fuck youself. He'll be here in a little while. Said he has business he wants to discuss. Can't wait."

"What're the chances of getting some breakfast?"

"Fifty-fifty. My cook is running late. Should be here soon."

Minutes after I settled into a back booth, my brother, Anthony, Tommy Cisco, and Sal Lomascio walked through the door.

"Mind if we join you?" Dave said.

I slid over to make room. "Swell! Breakfast with the family."

Dave appeared to be in a good mood, and Cisco had his wiseass sneer firmly in place. But Anthony's dour look told me he wasn't having a particularly sparkling day.

"Better!" my brother said. "This is a celebration."

"What's the occasion?"

Nick brought over a fresh pot of coffee and four mugs. He looked at Dave and then at Anthony, shook his head, and disappeared back behind the bar.

"The DA is throwing out the bullshit felony murder indictment. And they don't have enough to link me to the arson, either."

"How'd you find out?"

"Got a guy in the DA's office. Called my lawyer. The mope who bought it in Coney Island clinched it."

"Remember him well."

"Me and Sal were in Atlantic City when the poor bastard got sliced and diced. I got the receipts to prove it."

"That's great news, Dave."

"Like I said, it's a celebration. And now you can walk away from Martine and get on with your life."

"Assuming she lets me."

"I heard about that little incident you had. Almost took you out. Warned you about them, didn't I?"

"You did. But you should have warned Luce, too."

"I'm not following."

"Thanks to your pal Terry Sloan, she's facing a departmental trial."

Dave rubbed his cheek with the stump of his hand.

"I didn't see that coming," he said. "The slimy fuck put you out on the plank. But he's about to take your place."

"Doesn't help Luce."

"Because you don't do real well at listening."

"Not my long suit, Dave. I guess in that way we're a lot alike."

"Isn't the only way," he said.

"Actually, it is."

"Whatever," he said with a shrug. "And Anthony here, he isn't too good at listening either." Dave looked at his son, sitting directly across from him. "Are you, kid?"

The celebration was over.

Anthony had wrapped his hands around the mug so tightly his fingers twitched. Cisco just sat there with a shit-eating grin, taking it all in.

"Why don't you lay off him?"

"Lay off? Here's what happens when I leave my son to his own devices. I put money on the street. I send my son out to collect. Easy job. Right? Not for Anthony. He comes back short."

Anthony stared down at his coffee. "Only one guy," he said. "Just one. A hundred and fifty dollars. Not a big deal."

Dave slammed his hand down on the table so hard the mugs danced.

"It's *my* business!" Dave shouted. "Who the hell are you to make that decision?"

"I'm outta here," Sal said, rising from his chair. "I'll be in touch, Dave."

Anthony struggled to keep his voice low. "The guy's life is a shambles. Lost his job. His apartment. He's living out of his car. I know. I saw it. A heap. Tires are flat. How's he going to come up with the money?"

"He tells you a sob story, and you buy it. And I'm supposed to give a shit. He lives in his car. I own it. Oh, I forgot. You're out of the car-stealing business, 'cause you fucked that up too."

Anthony reached into his pocket, came out with a fistful of bills, and threw them in Dave's face. I wanted to applaud.

Anthony got up from the table. "That'll cover his next couple of installments," he said. "I'm through here."

Cisco would have made it out of Feeney's intact. If he just hadn't laughed. It wasn't much. A muffled giggle. Tops.

But it was enough.

Dave's cheek glowed a dark red. Something terrible was coming. And I didn't move fast enough to stop it.

Dave grabbed the glass coffeepot by the handle and drove it into Cisco's face. His head slammed back against the seat, and a long *oooooh!* came out of his mouth.

Anthony went pale. When he finally mustered the energy to speak, he had only one question.

"Why . . . ?"

Dave didn't wait for him to finish.

"The organ grinder's monkey should know better to laugh at the man who feeds him bananas," he said.

As if there were a spill on the table that needed attention, Dave waved Nick over. "Clean up this mess."

"I'm calling an ambulance," Nick said.

"Fine. Have them pick him up outside. Anthony can go along for the ride."

"It's below zero and snowing again," Nick said.

"Let's hope the EMT guys don't run into traffic."

There was no point to arguing. Nick and Anthony helped Cisco out to the street.

"Nicely done, Dave. You keep this up and Anthony's going to explode. Won't be pretty."

"Got to set an example. Else how's the kid gonna learn?"

"Maybe he doesn't like your method of instruction."

"Not your business."

"It is when he takes a swing at me."

Dave looked surprised. "He hit you?"

"Put me on the ground when I suggested that he get as far away from you as possible."

"So he knocked you on your ass, huh?" he said with a proud smile. "Maybe there's still hope for him."

"You know, the older you get the more you sound like Pop."

"Nah. He would've taken a more direct approach."

Hard to argue with.

"Remember when after the explosion . . . ," Dave gestured unconsciously with his stump, "I was laid up."

"I do."

"I'm laying on the bed, full of painkillers, and everyone thinks I'm out of it. Don't know what's going on. But I heard everything."

"Like what?"

"Like Anthony saying he was going to kill that fucking Hebe. And Franny whacking him in the mouth and telling him it ends here."

"Good memory."

"There's more. You telling everyone that I was sorry, when what I really said was the sins of the father are visited on the children."

"So I edited it a touch."

"And you were right to do it. And so was Franny. The craziness should have ended for Anthony in that hospital room. It didn't. And that's on me."

"And your point?"

"We both know this has nothing to do with Cisco, don't we, Jake?"

"I'm not following."

"A few weeks ago you nail Cisco with a right that would bring down a hippo. And today I rearrange his face. Cisco is nothing to us. Dirt under our fingernails. So the question is, why?"

"I was pissed."

"At who? Not at Cisco, who we both agree isn't worth our energy."

"Anthony," I said.

"Bingo! But you love my kid too much to kick the crap out of him. So you take it out on Cisco. Me too. See, you and me, we're not too different after all."

It was a troubling thought.

"Now you're going Freudian on me."

"Whatever. If my son would take his head out of his ass, he would see what my life has cost me. But Anthony seems to think this is romantic, and we're a bunch of happy-go-lucky swashbucklers."

"And you want to disabuse him of that notion through your supremely fucked-up version of tough love."

Dave nodded. "Before he thinks of becoming a boss, he's got to see what it's like to be a worker. A wad of chewing gum stuck on the bottom of his boss's shoe. Maybe then he'll realize what a shitty life this is."

"And if he doesn't figure it out?"

"What's to figure? Unless he finds another line of work, he's damned. Just like his old man."

28

By the time I made it out to the street, the ambulance had come and gone. But the half-dollar-sized snowflakes spitting down from a roof of gray-bellied clouds hadn't. Gusty crosswinds sent them spinning. Kenny Apple stood in the middle of the maelstrom, leaning on his car and blowing on his hands.

"Why're you out in the middle of a blizzard?" I said.

He jutted his chin at Feeney's. "A lot more congenial than in there."

Hard to argue with.

"You look like shit," I said.

"Had to kill a man last night. Takes something out of you."

"For my brother?"

"For you.

"Who?"

"His driver's license said John Riley."

"What happened?"

"You spent the night with Allie."

"When you left, you said you were gonna take a nap."

"It's more fun chasing after you. So I figured I'd hang around a bit. See what they'd do."

"And what did they do?"

"Riley pulls into a spot across the street from her building, sees the two of you go in, and sits in his car for about five hours. I guess he got bored waiting for you to make an appearance. Opened the door and came out with a semiautomatic. It was late. The street was empty, so the dumb bastard didn't even try to hide it."

"And?"

"He crossed the street and was almost at the curb when I put a bullet in his head. Went down between two parked cars. No muss. No fuss. I pulled over, stuffed him in the trunk of my car, and dropped him in the weeds out near JFK."

Kenny handed me Riley's wallet.

"Without this," he said, "the cops will have to run his prints, and it'll take longer to identify him. That should give us more time to deal with the other half of the dynamic duo before he knows there's something wrong."

I took Riley's wallet and slipped it into my pocket.

"I owe you, Kenny," I said. "What can I do to repay you?"

"Take a ride with me."

"Where?"

"I've got a terrible yen to see my kids."

• • •

Yeshiva Ohel Joseph, on Ocean Parkway in Brooklyn, was an imposing three-story building faced in mammoth slabs of beige stone. Snow decorated the flat places like icing on a cake.

Kenny parked the car on a side street across from the schoolyard, checked his watch, and settled in.

"What are we waiting for?" I said.

"My wife to pick them up. This way I get to see the three of them."

"Why don't you just go in?"

"Sarah has an order of protection. Can't go within a hundred yards of my own children."

"Your wife really knows how to carry a grudge."

Kenny shrugged. "She's right. Didn't want a killer anywhere near her kids."

"How long were you married?"

"Twelve very good years," he said. "And then I threw it all away. Turned into the man I was always meant to be."

"From where I sit, you're one of the best men I know."

"No, I'm not. We all have a destiny. I'm living it. And it's not pretty. "

"Don't you think you're being a little hard on yourself?

"Self-flagellation is the only thing that keeps me going."

"What's my destiny, Kenny?"

"You'll figure it out." He shifted around in his seat.

"You know, I still love her. Always will. She's the one who got the raw deal. Not me."

"Now you're feeling sorry for yourself."

"And that's one of the other things I do really well." He straightened up. "There she is, out front. And there're the kids."

Kenny opened the door and got out of the car. I got out of the car with him.

I hurried up to him.

"Where're you going?"

"To hug my kids."

"What about the order of protection?"

"What can a judge do to me that I haven't done to myself?"

"I don't know if this is such a good idea," I said.

He smiled. "What's that you always say? In for a dime, in for a dol—"

And then everything happened in a blur of quick cuts.

A car bearing down on us.

Kenny yelling my name. Shoving me to the ground.

An explosion.

Kenny's muffled grunt.

His body spinning, and finally falling on top of mine.

The cops and the ambulance arrived at about the same time. The cops took my statement while the EMT guys tended to Kenny. I told them the truth. I saw nothing and heard little more. When everyone was finished and all the notepads were put away, I hopped on the ambulance and rode with Kenny to Maimonides Medical Center.

"Hell of a note, isn't it, Steeg?" he gasped from the stretcher.

A fine sheen of sweat covered his face, and his skin was the color of ash.

"Hell of a note," I agreed. "How're you doing?"

"Feels like someone took a hacksaw to my shoulder."

"You're lucky I'm not fitting you for a toe tag," one of the EMT guys said.

"A cheery thought," Kenny said.

"No, it's a fact," the EMT guy said. "When we get to the hospital, the docs'll dig the slug out, and in a couple of days or so you'll be good to go."

He checked Kenny's dressing. "Look's like the bleeding's under control," he said. "I've got some paperwork to do." He pointed to a spot near the driver. "If you need me, holler."

"I keep running up a tab with you, Kenny," I said.

"Big-time," he said, wincing as the ambulance hit a bump.

"Fucking potholes!" the driver said.

"Did my wife and kids see what happened, Steeg?"

Tough question to answer since my view of pretty much everything had been blocked by Kenny's body lying on top of mine. But I gave Kenny the only answer that would give him some measure of peace.

"I don't think so. Everyone scattered."

"Thank God for small blessings," he said. "Now what?"

"You rest up for a while. Heal. And you'll be fine."

"That's not what I was talking about. That crazy fucker is hell-bent on blowing you away. And you don't have me to watch your back."

"Maybe it's time to do some hunting of my own."

29

While I waited for Kenny to come out of surgery, I got a call from Nick.

"Steeg, someone came by looking for you," he said.

"Was he carrying a piece?"

"What're you talking about?"

"I'm at Maimonides Medical Center in Borough Park. Kenny just took a bullet for me."

His voice was low. "He gonna make it?"

"Shoulder is all messed up. Docs are working on him now. But, yeah. He'll be fine."

"What the hell were you doing in Brooklyn?"

"Kenny wanted to see his kids. I tagged along. Happened right outside their school."

"That's truly fucked. Who did it? The two psychos who were in here a while ago?"

"Yep. Or one of them at least. Kenny took the other one out last night. Dumped his body out near Kennedy."

"Nice. But I prefer Rockland County. Lots of wooded areas. Guys I stashed there twenty years ago still haven't been found."

"You always were a purist."

"If something's worth doing, it's worth doing right."

"Words to live by," I said. "Look, I need a favor."

"Name it."

"Kenny blew him away outside Allie's apartment house. It doesn't take Charlie Chan to figure out that Ennis now knows where she lives."

"And you want someone to sort of watch over her."

"Surreptitiously. She can't know that she's being guarded. Allie kind of pushes back when I'm being overly protective."

"And that someone would be me."

"Will you do it?"

"In a heartbeat. Allie won't even know I'm around."

"Perfect. Now, let's get back to the individual who was looking for me."

"Make her for a hooker. Said her name is Gloria. Dawn's friend. Gave me her number. You want it?"

We met at a ragged-around-the-edges Times Square bar that years ago began life as a jazz club. Now it catered to tourists and conventioneers looking to get laid.

Gloria sat at a table in the back nursing a beer. She'd cleaned up some since I had seen her at Dawn's apartment.

I took a seat opposite her.

"How'd you know where to find me?" I said.

"Your card. You gave it to Dawn. Remember? Never heard of somebody usin' a saloon as a business address."

"Unfortunately, it's where I spend most of my time."

She shrugged. "Different strokes."

"What happened to Dawn?" I said.

"Martine happened to her."

"Care to expand on that?"

"Dawn and Martine go way back," she said. "Never did like each other. Rickie saw that Martine was doing real good and . . ."

"Tried to shake her down."

"That's about it. Fuckin' Rickie thought it was a great idea. Said he could handle things if they got rough. Well, they got real rough." She looked up at the bar and called out, "Where the hell is my beer?"

The bartender threw her a look.

"Fuckin' place!" she said.

"Let's get back to Martine and Dawn."

"So Rickie says a hundred large. Gonna be the score of a lifetime. Get us out of this fuckin' city. Go someplace warm. The three of us." She shook her head. "Rickie always had somethin' workin'. Asshole!"

"So Dawn threatened to expose Another Chance as a prostitution ring. Martine luring the girls in with promises of a new life, and selling their bodies to the rich and famous."

"And freaky. Shoulda known better than to screw with people like that."

The bartender brought the beer over and thumped the bottle on the table.

"Jerkoff," she muttered. "Where was I? Oh yeah, a couple of days after you dropped by, Martine's apes show up."

"Where were you?"

"Out in the street. Comin' back from a . . . business meeting, y'know? Anyway, I seen Martine's boyfriend Ennis and the other guy draggin' Dawn and Rickie out of the building and stuffing them in a car. Last I seen of them."

"What'd you do?"

"Got my shit out of the apartment and split. That's where I found your card. Dawn threw it into a drawer."

"What now?"

She smiled. "Found Rickie's stash while I was packin'. Enough to get me to Vegas."

I laid a twenty on the table to pay for the beers.

There was no point mourning for Dawn. I had done that years ago.

I pushed the chair back and got to my feet. "Thanks for clearing things up."

"There's more."

I sat back down.

"You asked Dawn about a workin' girl who'd be pissed off enough to ice some johns."

"I did."

"There's one that Dawn and I used to talk about. The life truly fucks you up, but with this girl it went overboard.

Used to work for Martine. Saved her for the real fuckin' sickos. If anyone fit your bill, it would be her. I know where she is and can get you to her."

"Why're you doing this?"

"Dawn said you were a good guy. She figured that Rickie had his head up his ass with his scheme. And she knew how it would turn out."

"But she went along anyway?"

"Choice was a rock and a hard place. Martine or Rickie. Either way she lost. She figured maybe you'd see what Martine was up to and put her out of business."

"She was right, but her timing was off."

"Life can be a bitch."

"This girl have a name?"

"Only her street name," she said. "Randi."

30

Turns out my meeting wasn't with Randi, but with a woman named Tiffany. And I was instructed to bring five hundred dollars.

I met her at a diner near Penn Station. The place reeked of bacon grease. An old man with a milky eye and a goiter as big as an orange repeatedly dipped his mop into a pail full of dark gray water and swished at the slop that customers tracked into the restaurant. It was a losing proposition.

Tiffany was a tall black woman who used lots of peroxide on her hair and a heavy hand on her makeup. She looked to be in her early thirties, but I guessed her age at ten years younger. The life tends to wear you down.

"Got the money?" she said.

On my way to the diner, I'd tapped an ATM for five hundred. That left a hundred and twenty-seven until the next pension check hit my account. I pulled out a wad of twenties and fanned them on the table. Her eyes actually dilated.

"If you've got Randi," I said.

"I do."

"Will she talk to me?"

"For another five."

"For you, or for her?"

She smiled.

"A girl's got to make a living," she said.

"OK. Where is she?"

"I'll take you to her."

"When?"

"First thing in the morning." Tiffany wrote the address on a napkin and slipped it across the table. "Randi's working tonight and got to earn. Gonna be a full night."

"You're pimping her."

"More like her booking agent. But we're doing the gig together. Bachelor party. Bunch of Wall Street types. And we're the headliners."

"No business like show business."

Tiffany shrugged.

"Pays the rent," she said.

"Randi know about our little arrangement?"

"Not yet. But she won't have a problem."

"Why's that?"

"We have a special relationship."

"I can see that. She takes the risks, and you get the rewards."

"It ain't what you think," Tiffany said. "We love each

other. We're saving up and getting the hell out of this business. Gonna find a little place upstate, and it'll just be the two of us."

The snakes in my head stirred. I knew I was close to blowing the deal, but the words came anyway.

"Yeah. With a white picket fence and rosebushes, and maybe a collie to romp around the yard," I said. "Give me a fucking break!"

"It's not like that."

"Yeah, it is. Don't give me this *love* shit. You're a pimp, and that's all she wrote."

"Randi is sick. Real sick. After the fire that killed her sister, she ran. And I took her in. Ain't gonna be much more work for either of us. And I bought the place. Up in Rochester. Where I'm from. *Both* our names are on the deed. Show it to you if you like. No collie. No fence. And I don't know shit about rosebushes."

"Sick, as in AIDS?"

"Breast cancer. Real advanced. Just a matter of time now. The docs wanted to do a double mastectomy, but Randi said no. We needed money for the down payment." Her voice turned bitter. "And a whore without tits is not a big attraction."

The snakes went back to their slumber.

"I'm sorry," I said. "If there's anything I can do . . ."

"Our problem. No one else's. And we're dealing with it best we know how." She put the bills in a stack and jammed them in her pocketbook. "And this is gonna help. Our line of work don't pay benefits."

"There are other doctors. Have you—?"

"Been to a bunch of them. All say the same thing. A year. Maybe less. Nothing more they can do for Wanda. My turn now."

A bubble of white heat traveled up from my brain stem and settled just behind my eyes.

"Randi's name is Wanda?"

"Wanda Klemper. Funny, ain't it?"

Not from where I sat.

31

amon Runyon, one of the most perceptive observers of the human condition, once said, "I long ago came to the conclusion that life is six to five against." For Wanda and Angela Klemper, the odds were off the board.

Birth to death in a few short, terrible years, and everyone responsible gets to skate. Kind of makes you wonder about a beneficent God and His magic wand of redemption.

And it makes you want to make someone pay.

I needed Allie to snap me out of my melancholy. But even though Nick was babysitting her, with Martine and Ennis still out there, my presence would have put her at risk.

I compromised by calling her. Just to check in.

"Hi," I said. "How're you doing?"

"Things are settling back to normal. In a fashion."

"Meaning?"

"How would you like to have dinner at my place tonight?"

With Nick outside playing Cerberus the three-headed dog, it was worth the risk.

"A sterling idea," I said. "Let's order in. I've got a yen for Mexican."

"Won't be necessary. Dinner is going to be a surprise."

"You're cooking?"

"A lady has to have some secrets. See you at seven."

I went home. Cleaned my Glock and loaded it. Dropped it, along with an extra clip, in my jacket pocket. Took a shower and a quick nap. And was out the door by six thirty, stopping only to pick up a dozen roses at Benny Kim's establishment.

The hallway outside Allie's apartment had the intense, garlicky aroma of a neighborhood Italian restaurant.

She greeted me at the door with a chaste peck on the lips.

"They're lovely, Steeg," she said, taking the flowers. "Make yourself comfortable while I put them in water."

I walked into the living room while Allie went to fetch a vase.

"So this is where the perfume's coming from," I said.

"It is."

"But you don't know how to cook."

"That's the surprise. I engaged a chef just for tonight."

"You're kidding."

"Would you like to meet him?"

"Sure."

She took my hand and led me into the kitchen, where Nick, looking for all the world like a crazed incarnation of Chef Boyardee, was laboring at the stove. "What in hell are you doing here?" I said.

"What's it look like I'm doing? You got veal and peppers, chicken cacciatore, sautéed arugula, linguini, garlic bread in the oven, and a salad of tomatoes and thinly sliced red onion. Lotta dishes working. Is there a problem?"

"Yeah. You were supposed to be invisible. What happened?"

"It was freezing outside, and I felt like a putz standing around in the lobby," Nick said. "So I went up to the agency."

I looked at Allie.

"I'm really sorry," I said. "But . . . y' know . . . I was worried about you."

"That was very thoughtful, Steeg. And Nick was, for the most part, discreet."

"What do you mean, *for the most part*?"

"Other than hitting on every woman in the place, Nick was the model of decorum. He was a really big hit with one of my clients. Apparently, she found him charming."

"Yeah," Nick said. "As soon as this thing with you blows over, I could see the possibilities of a relationship. Nice gal. Great body."

I turned to Nick.

"I asked you to do one simple thing, and you screw it up."

"What's screwed up? Allie's safe, isn't she? And I may have stumbled across the next Mrs. D'Amico. The way I see it, it's a win-win all around."

"Lovely," I said.

I took a fork from the counter, speared a piece of chicken from the pot, and popped it into my mouth.

"I were you, I'd fire your cook and take over Feeney's kitchen. You'd make a fortune."

"Their taste buds are so far gone, the rummies who frequent my joint would never know the difference."

Fair point.

"So," Nick continued, "why don't we all sit down to eat?"

We ladled the food onto our plates and brought them into the dining alcove. Allie contented herself with a slice of tomato and a few onion shards.

"Nick told me Kenny was in the hospital," Allie said.

I threw Nick a look. Allie knew the work I did sometimes involved an element of risk, but the details were never up for discussion.

Nick gave an almost imperceptible shake of his head and poured himself a glass of Chianti.

"He'll be fine," I said. "Should be home in a few days."

"Good," Allie said. "I like him, but I don't understand him. I mean how does an observant Jew work for someone like your brother?"

"Everybody's gotta do something," Nick said, ripping off a hunk of garlic bread and plunging it into the sauce. "Besides, I work for Dave too."

"But you're . . ."

Nick put down the bread, and his voice went hard. "A thug, and Kenny's not?" Nick said.

Nick was never very big on nuance.

"That's not what I meant," Allie said. "Kenny wears his faith on his sleeve, while you're at least consistent."

Nick smiled, and reached over and patted her hand.

"Was there a compliment in there?"

"Most assuredly so. And the fact you gave up your time to protect me from being collateral damage at the hands of whoever is trying to kill Steeg only makes me like you more."

"What makes you think someone is trying to kill me?" I said.

"Let's see. When I left my apartment this morning, Nick is lurking around up the block. I walked to the subway and he's right behind me, as inconspicuous as a rhino. And then he shows up at the agency with some cockamamie story about how he's thinking of doing some advertising for Feeney's and wants to learn how the business works. *Please!*"

"I guess tailing isn't one of my long suits."

This time Nick at least had the decency to look ashamed of himself.

Allie impaled a slice of tomato and diced it into half-inch pieces.

"So," she said, "pray tell, who's trying to kill you, Steeg, and why?"

I wasn't about to go there.

"What's going on in your world, Nick?"

"Your brother's stepping up the pressure on Anthony."

"It sounds very Oedipal," Allie said.

"More like immigrant shanty Irish," I chimed in. "The kids do better than the parents, and so on. In a couple or three generations you have the Kennedys. Bootlegger to President. In a way, that's what Dave wants for Anthony."

"And look what it got old Joe," Nick said.

"But the dream remains."

"Not for your brother. Anthony took a swing at him."

"Not surprised."

"Fucker deserved it. Dave was all over him for some bullshit thing Anthony did or didn't do. Who knows? Anyway, the kid lost it and threw a punch."

"How did Dave handle it?"

"He grabbed his hand in midair and held it for a bit. I thought he was going to kick the shit out of him, but he just walked away."

"Dave could never hit Anthony," I said. "Never lifted a hand to any of his kids. Franny was the disciplinarian."

"It's Oedipal," Allie repeated. "For some reason he wants to hurt his father."

"*Hurt* is putting a really fine point on things, don't you think? As I recall, Oedipus killed his father."

32

Tiffany and Wanda shared an apartment on 130th Street and Riverside Drive in one of those prewar buildings that sported high ceilings, ornate wall moldings, and long-faded grandeur.

Tiffany, her face scrubbed clean of makeup, wore a loose-fitting neon blue warm-up suit. She met me at the door with a cup of black coffee in her hand.

"We had a rough night, so go easy on her," she said. "The shitheads made sure they got their money's worth."

"No problem. Couple of questions, and I'm gone."

"Got the rest of the money?"

Thanks to Nick, I did. And he even let the interest slide.

I pressed the bills into her hand.

She slipped them into her jacket pocket and motioned me in.

I followed her into the tiny kitchen, where Wanda, wearing an off-white terry-cloth robe, sat at the table nursing a glass of orange juice. Her lusterless light brown hair was pulled back in a ponytail secured by a rubber band. The dull, glazed look in her eyes told me that she had spent an evening in the company of The Beast, and wasn't ready for another go-around anytime soon.

Tiffany moved behind Wanda and gently stroked the nape of her neck.

"Wanda, honey," she said. "This is Steeg. Remember? I told you about him?"

In an attitude that almost resembled prayer, Wanda's hands were splayed palms up on the table. She kept her eyes fixed on them as if the answers to all the mysteries of the world could be read in their lines and creases.

I took a seat at the table. Tiffany sat between us.

"Wanda, do you know why I'm here?"

She shook her head.

"Last Christmas Eve there was a terrible fire at a warehouse in Hell's Kitchen. Three bodies were found on the main floor. One of them was your sister, Angela."

Wanda nodded again. "I was there," she said, in a voice that sounded like it had snaked up from the bottom of a gravel pit.

It was one of those electric moments when the burden suddenly lightens and the world is righted on its axis.

"At the warehouse?"

Wanda nodded again.

"It was snowing like hell," she said. "Business was

lousy. Didn't want to go back to my apartment with nothing to show for it and get my ass kicked again. So I found a bar and settled in." Her eyes filled with tears. "And then Angela called."

"Where was she?"

"Said she was in a warehouse with two guys. They were having a party. Said she missed me."

"How long had it been since you'd seen her?"

Tiffany reached over and patted Wanda's cheeks dry with a napkin. Wanda took it from her and crumpled it in her fist.

"Couple of months," she said. "And it's my fault she's dead. Now it's my turn. Guess we all have to pay, don't we? Only right."

"Why do you think it's your fault?"

"Angela ran from those bastards because of me. And wound up dead because of me."

"Which bastards are we talking about?"

"The mother who squeezed me out of her body twenty-three years ago, and her rat bastard husband who belted me and Angie around whenever he had a yen."

"Jonas wasn't your father?"

"My real father skipped when Angie came along. Hardly remember him."

She took her eyes off her hands and fixed them on me.

"How did you know his name was Jonas?" she said.

"I met him. Met them both. They came here to have Angela's body shipped back home."

She went back to studying her hands, her voice a monotone. "They're the ones who deserve to be dead. Fucking monsters. She knew what he was doing, and let it happen. And him? I'll never forget the look on his face when he hit us. I swear the bastard got off on it."

Tiffany took Wanda's hand in hers and held it tight.

"It's over, baby," she cooed. "They can't hurt you no more."

"But I'm going to hurt them. If it's the last thing I do."

I could only wish her well.

"Let's get back to Angela," I said. "A few minutes ago you said you were responsible for her death."

"I was. I had some money saved that they didn't know about. I could have sent it to her, and she could have gone somewhere safe. But they made me bring her here. Told me what would happen to me if I didn't get her to come to New York."

"Who made you?"

"Martine and Ennis. Said they would send me to Asia or some other place, and I'd never come back. I believed them. It happened to other girls. And no one ever heard from them again. So I did what I was told."

Tiffany nodded. "Show Steeg what she did to you, honey."

Wanda undid the belt of her robe and shrugged it off. A tattoo of a tarot card adorned her left breast.

The snakes in my head whirled like dervishes.

"All of Martine's girls had them," Tiffany said. "Part of the deal when you worked for her."

Wanda snorted a bitter rattle that was meant to be a laugh.

"I didn't know that at first. I was working for this pimp who enjoyed tearing me up in ways I didn't think possible. I heard about Martine from some other girls. Said she would help me get out of the life. See, that's how she recruited."

She took a sip of orange juice and continued.

"So I went to see Martine. Told her my story. And she took me in. Set me up in a fancy apartment. Bought me new clothes. Plenty of food in the refrigerator. Told me not to worry about a thing. Everything's gonna to be just fine."

"And then she lowered the boom."

"Oh yeah. Ennis shows up. Worse than my first pimp. Smacks me around, rapes me, and then reads me the new Gospel according to Saint Martine."

"Church of the Holy Buck," Tiffany muttered.

"All the johns were these rich, important guys," Wanda said. "But they were just creepy, fucking johns. Don't even know how they came up with the things they wanted me to do. Didn't even ask for us by our own names. Just by whatever our tarot card name was."

"What was the name of your card?"

Wanda turned away.

"The Fool," she said. "Kinda fits, don't it?"

Wanda stared at a spot on the far wall. Her eyes were dull and empty.

"Did you see Angela at the warehouse?"

"I never made it inside. Flames were shooting out all over."

She paused.

"There's something else," she said. "About the fire. Something I saw."

I waited for her to continue.

"A man standing across the street. Just watching the fire eat up that building." She looked down at her hands again. "And everything in it."

It was time to take things slow and easy.

"What did he look like, Wanda?"

"The Devil."

"Can you describe him?"

"White guy. Big. Heavyset. Wearing a parka with one of those hoods."

"How about his hair? Blond? Dark? Long? Short?"

"Didn't see. Had the hood up. Just his face. Got a good look at that."

"Anything special about it? Any marks? Scars?"

"No."

"About how old was he?"

"Hard to tell," she said. "Twenties. Maybe thirty. Maybe less. Just saw him for a second or two. He saw me. Stared at me. I was so scared, I ran."

"What frightened you?"

"The look on his face. Like Death."

"Get your money's worth, Steeg?" Tiffany asked.

"Much more. Do you have any idea where Martine and Ennis are now, Wanda?"

"They have a hidey-hole up in Harlem, I think. New building. I heard Ennis bragging about it to Riley. Liked the idea that they were living high on the hog and could look out the window and as far as the eye could see, everyone else was living in shit."

"Got an address?"

"No."

"Doesn't matter. I'll find them."

"And when you do?"

"Gonna send them your regards."

33

This assignment was right up Kenny's alley. Unfortunately, he was temporarily out of commission. That left one other possibility.

I called my brother and told him to meet me at Feeney's.

When I arrived, he was already there, sitting in his customary back booth with a bottle of Johnny Black for company.

He lifted his half-empty glass and drained it. "Your meeting," he said.

I slid in opposite him.

"So much for fraternal warmth," I said. "Where's your alter ego?"

"Anthony? Beats me."

"I hear the two of you were at it again."

"Bad news travels fast."

"When's it gonna end, Dave? You can't keep hammering him."

He shrugged.

"That's the thing he's got to understand."

"What thing?"

"Hammering a square peg in a round hole just doesn't work."

"Why not sit him down and quietly tell him that he's not cut out for your business?"

"How do you fire your own kid?"

"Be a problem if you ran a normal business. But you don't."

"Enough of this bullshit. Why're you here?"

"I need your help," I said.

He flashed me a cold smile.

"Now the tone changes and the bitching about what a shitty father I am goes away. Nice."

I made a move out of the booth.

"Go fuck yourself, Dave."

His hand shot across the table and latched onto my jacket.

"Don't go," he said.

"Why not? You're crazier than a March hare. And being in your company is a trial."

His grip loosened.

"Just don't," he said.

It was the same small, frightened voice I remembered hearing when we were kids and he was terrified of the dark. Dominic would kick Dave out when he tried to crawl between him and Norah. And he wound up spending the night in my bed.

I settled back in my seat.

"What's happening to you, Dave?" I said. "You're turning into something straight out of a Shakespearean tragedy."

He rubbed his cheek with the stump of his hand.

"Everything's haywire," he said. "Hard to figure out which end is up anymore."

I reached for his good hand. "You've got to hold it together, Dave."

"I don't give a shit anymore."

"I need you to snap out of this funk you're in."

"It's the only thing left that gives me pleasure."

"Remember when we were kids and someone messed with me?"

"A mistake they wouldn't make twice."

"Looks like I need your help again."

The transformation was astounding. My brother was reborn. He sat up straighter, and the color was back in his face. It was as if I had dipped him in a baptismal fount and all of his troubles just washed away. Even his voice was stronger.

"Martine?"

"You're still running numbers banks up in Harlem, right?"

"And?"

I told him about Wanda and Martine and Ennis, and the business they were in.

"Pretty slick," he said. "Every time you think there are no new ideas, one pops up."

"I'm sure Martine would appreciate your admiration."

"Should've been working for me. Instead, I got Anthony."

It was the first time in months I had seen him this animated.

He waved Nick over. "You gotta hear this," he said.

When Dave had finished extolling Martine's marketing prowess, Nick was unimpressed.

"We don't run hookers," he said. "Not our business."

Nick was right. Prostitution wasn't Dave's business. The only time he'd dabbled in the flesh trade, he came up against the Law of Unintended Consequences. And it resulted in the death of a half sister we never knew we had.

"Yeah, but it doesn't make this Martine any less of a genius," Dave said.

"Whatever," Nick said, losing enthusiasm for the conversation.

"You never were big on imagination, Nick," Dave said.

"If I were, I'd be in another line of work."

"Can't argue with that. Anyway, Jake here needs our help." He turned to me. "Tell him who you're looking for."

"Martine Toussaint, and her boyfriend Frank Ennis. Martine has a heavy duty Haitian accent. Wears her hair in dreadlocks. Ennis you know. They live together in a luxury high-rise somewhere in Harlem."

"That narrows it down," Nick said.

"Can't have everything. Anyway, could you put the word out to the bankers and their networks that we're looking for them, and willing to pay?"

"How much?"

"I've got a little over a hundred in my bank account," I said.

"Dollars?"

"Available immediately."

"Let's see," Nick said. "Snake-mean black gal. White boyfriend armed to the teeth. And a hundred bucks for the guy who rats 'em out. Who wouldn't jump at that?"

"Make it five large," Dave said. "The money comes from my pocket. You tell them *I* need it done. And if there's any push back, you let me know."

Nick nodded.

"All's I need is an address," I said. "I'll take it from there."

"Alone?" Dave asked.

"It's what I had in mind."

"Want some help?"

"From who?"

"Me. And Nick comes along for backup."

"Could be an adventure," Nick said. "Haven't had one of those in a while."

"Then it's settled," Dave said.

"Why're you doing this?"

He lifted Johnny B and slammed one back straight from the bottle.

"It'll be just like old times," Dave said. "The Steeg boys together again. And screw 'em all!"

Just like old times.

As I recalled, that's what got me into this mess in the first place.

"I almost forgot," Nick said. "DeeDee came by looking for you. She was with her boyfriend. Anyway, between you and me, I didn't like the way they were acting."

"Define *acting*."

"Y'know, all cuddly, and kissy face. Stuck together like someone poured Krazy Glue on them."

"Someone new, or Justin, the kid she's been seeing?"

"The old boyfriend," Nick said. "Have you talked to her about . . . ?"

"About what?"

"You know. Boys. And what assholes they are."

"Nick has a point," Dave said. "She's a young girl. You gotta let her know what the deal is."

It was like living in a lunatic asylum.

To exorcise the demons that persuaded him to turn parenting into cage fighting, Dave wants to paint the town with blood. And Nick, another wonderful role model for his kids, thinks murder would be an adventure. Then, as quick as a wink, the two nominees for Father of the Year weigh in on the responsibilities of parenthood.

"I'll get right on it, Dr. Spock."

34

eaving Dave and Nick to deal with the hobgoblins partying in their heads, I stopped in at DeeDee's apartment.

DeeDee answered my knock.

She and Justin weren't exactly in a state of deshabille. But close.

Her blouse was four buttons short of where it should have been. And Justin wasn't in much better shape. He sat on the sofa with his shirttails hanging out, and a troubled look on his face.

"There was a reason buttonholes were invented," I said.

DeeDee's face turned crimson.

She half-turned, her fingers quickly moving to her blouse. When she faced me again, she looked as prim and collected as a schoolmarm.

And I was the misbehaving child.

"Well," she said. "It's about time you showed up. I can't spend my time worrying about you, Steeg. It's not fair."

I shook my head in wonder.

"I'll try to do better in the future," I said.

Justin, who had yet to move, threw me a limp wave.

"So," DeeDee said, continuing to pile on, "where have you been?"

"Making the world safe for democracy."

"So that's how it's going to go."

"Pretty much."

"How come you don't let me in, Steeg?"

"Have you and Allie been comparing notes?"

"We care about you."

"And I care about you, kiddo. But some things are better left unsaid."

And that's where we left it.

I rubbed my hands together, trying to work some warmth into them.

"I know," DeeDee said. "The boiler's still on the fritz. My dad gets out in a few days, and he'll take care of it."

DeeDee's father was the building's super, and indisposed at the moment. A nice way of saying a bar fight had made him a guest of the city.

I settled in next to Justin and patted him on the knee.

"How goes it, kid?" I said.

"Y'know," he said. "Great. Just great."

The words were all in the right places, but lacked conviction.

"So, you two are an item again."

DeeDee came up and wedged herself between us.

"It was a silly argument about silly things," she said, looking at him adoringly. "But now it's behind us."

"Glad to hear it. And Justin, how's your dad?"

Something flickered across his face. And just as quickly, it was gone.

"He's, y'know, doing OK," he said.

"Nice guy. Seems to care about you."

Justin got up from the sofa.

"He's a loving man," Justin said. "Look, DeeDee. I've got to study. Got this biochem test tomorrow, and I still haven't figured out stereoisomerism."

He reached down to shake my hand. His hand was damp.

"Good to see you again, Mr. Steeg," he said. "Look forward to seeing you soon."

"You take care of yourself, Justin."

DeeDee walked him to the door, said her good-byes, then came back and snuggled in next to me.

"Are you happy for me, Steeg?"

"Deliriously so."

"Do you really mean it?"

I put my arm around her shoulder and hugged her tight.

"Every word of it."

"You're not just saying that to make me feel good?"

"You know, there are some people who think I didn't raise you right."

She pulled away.

"Who?"

"Nick, and my brother."

"Well their opinion has got to be worth absolutely nothing."

"They think I should have had the dreaded *talk* with you long before now."

"And what makes you think I need it?"

My eyes strayed to her blouse.

"Four buttons shy of modesty," I said.

"Nothing happened, Steeg. And even if it did, you can't fault us for being normal. It's all a matter of simple science. Biology and chemistry."

"With a soupçon of lust thrown in."

She smiled a wicked smile. "That's what makes it so exciting," she said.

"I'll make you a deal. I'll forgo the *talk* in exchange for a little honesty. OK?"

"Deal."

"From where I stood, it didn't look to me that *nothing* happened."

"Depends on your definition of nothing," she said.

"Are we having a presidential moment here?"

"Let's put it this way. Justin wanted something to happen. And I wanted something to happen. But he couldn't quite make it happen. From what I hear, it's perfectly normal. And that's as far as I'm going to go, so don't push it. I'm not going to get clinical with you."

"I mean, sometimes it takes a while to get everything—"

She threw her hands over her face.

"*Steeg!*"

"I'm just saying."

"Everything is going to work out just fine. Just say that you're happy for me."

"I'm happy for you."

I gave it my best shot, but my heart just wasn't in it.

35

Three days later I was on the Brooklyn Bridge, my favorite go-to spot for really deep reflection.

From the center of the span, 135 feet over the East River, things just seem to take on a different perspective. Even with the traffic flowing by and a whirling offshore wind plucking at the cables, there's an illusion of calm. A sense that all the bullshit of the world is filtered through the singing strings of a giant harp, and anything is possible.

But today the wind was strumming out a dirge.

For some reason I've never quite been able to figure out, there's a snowball effect to bad news. It begins as a couple of flakes of disappointment, and as it tumbles downhill it picks up annoyance, chagrin, distress, and a hunk of downright bewilderment along the way. And pretty soon, you've got a full-fledged avalanche.

With no else waiting in the wings, I had initially made someone like Wanda for the guys in the basement, and someone else for the torch. She fit my profile and hit the trifecta of means, motive, and opportunity. But I had it wrong. Wanda had no motive.

And she said she never made it inside.

Instead she claimed she saw someone—a very scary someone—standing outside watching.

And I believed her.

An arsonist-for-hire who didn't count on anyone being out and about on a snowy Christmas Eve? Nah. Dave didn't need the insurance money. And arsonists scoot long before the police show up.

A pyromaniac attracted to a deserted building and hanging around to enjoy his handiwork? Too far-fetched.

That left one other possibility. The heavyset, twenty-something guy Wanda saw *was* the murderer. And burned up his hidey-hole for reasons I couldn't possibly fathom.

Maybe my gay hustler theory was alive and kicking. He had motive, could've iced the guys in the basement and lit the warehouse up. But if that was what had happened, I was back at square one, with not a single lead.

And just when I thought things couldn't possibly get worse, Luce called. The NYPD forensic techs had found nothing illuminating or incriminating in Walter Cady's computer.

The snowball effect had definitely kicked in.

But maybe it was a good thing.

Dave was off the hook, the NYPD serial killer task

force was on the case, and there was nothing left for me to do.

Allie was back to her normal rhythms. Client budget cutbacks. Wall-to-wall meetings. Late nights. The usual stuff. DeeDee was dancing on clouds. Kenny was still in the hospital, but recovering. And my brother claimed that everything was cool between him and Anthony. At least for now.

And with Dave on the case, Martine would soon be run to ground.

But the best news of all was that DeeDee's father was out of the slam and working on the boiler.

Oh, there was one more thing. No one had tried to kill me in the last few days.

Kenny lay propped up in bed at a sixty-degree angle with his eyes half-closed. A curtain separated him from his roommate. The small television bolted to a high shelf on the far wall was tuned to a cable news channel. The audio was on mute. From where I stood, the news crawl at the bottom of the screen resembled sparrow tracks.

A beeping sound came from the other side of the curtain.

I pulled out the contents of a brown paper bag and laid them on the night table.

"Time for a snack, Kenny," I said. "Pastrami on rye with just the right amount of fat. Sour pickle. And a Dr. Brown's Cel-Ray to wash it all down. And it's all kosher."

He barely looked at the food.

"Not hungry," he said.

"That's a first. What's wrong? Are you in a lot of pain?"

He shook his head.

"Well, maybe your roommate's hungry?"

"After what he's been through?"

"What's his problem?"

"The guy is eighty-nine and just came out of quadruple bypass surgery. They cracked his chest. Attached his heart to a machine. Worked on him for hours. He's got so many tubes attached to him, when they wheeled him in he looked like he was entwined in latex vines."

I kept my voice real low. "I don't want to be a spoilsport," I said. "But at eighty-nine he doesn't have a whole hell of a lot of sand left in his hourglass. Why would he put himself through this?"

"For a woman. And you can speak up. The guy's so far out of it, they can lop off his limbs and he wouldn't know it."

"I'm not following the *woman* part."

"The nurses tell me he got married about a year ago. She's eighty-five. And wants a—how did they put it?—a robust sex life. But every time he tried to get *robust,* he thought his chest would explode. So here he is lying there like a lox."

"I wish them mazel tov."

Kenny made a face. "I'm sure he'd appreciate that. Not right now, but when he wakes up in six months and looks in the mirror and sees a schmuck staring back."

"The things we do for sex."

"The things we do for women," he said. "My wife came to visit me."

"Oh? How did that go?"

From the look on his face, not well.

"You didn't ask how come she knew I was here."

"I figured someone in your family called her."

"She saw what happened in front of the Yeshiva."

"I didn't know that. I figured she scattered with everyone else."

"No way you should. She came to pick up the kids and spotted my car. She was dialing 911 to have the cops haul me in for violating the restraining order when the gunfight at the OK Corral broke out."

"She told you this?"

He nodded. "Not a lot of sympathy there. She also told me that this was God's punishment for my profligate ways."

"She actually used the word *profligate*?"

"Oh yeah. Sarah's quite the wordsmith. English lit major at Brooklyn College. Read all the dead white guys. She went on to say that if she ever sees me near her or the kids again, she'll have me thrown so far into jail they'll have to feed me with a slingshot."

"And she knows how to turn a phrase, too," I said. "I'm really sorry I got you into this, Kenny."

"You didn't get me into anything. It's all on me. It's like they say. You've got to take ownership of your problems before you can solve them."

"It's the alcoholic's creed. So, what now?"

"The docs are releasing me tomorrow. Then it's back to an empty apartment and shooting people for profit. Welcome to my life, Steeg."

Further conversation was mercifully interrupted by the sound of my cell phone playing George Jones's classic "He Stopped Loving Her Today."

It seemed like the perfect sum-up.

36

The phone call was from Nick.

He and Dave were at the Yellow Dog, a Harlem after-hours club. He gave me the address. I hopped a train at Times Square.

Even with the address, finding the Yellow Dog turned out to be a chore. After I'd traversed the block twice with no luck, a very large black man with a gold medallion the size of a coffee table book dangling from his neck pointed to a door behind and below him.

The club consisted of a small bar against the back wall, about a dozen tables scattered about, a plywood band-stand, and no customers. It smelled like an ashtray.

Dave and Nick sat at a large round table with two black guys. One was in his fifties and morbidly obese. The other, wearing a Mets cap turned backward, was much younger and a hell of a lot leaner. The younger guy sat with his head in his heads.

Dave waved me over.

I took a seat next to him.

He skipped the introductions.

"What took you so long?" he said.

"Track problems. What's up?"

"I don't understand why you can't take a cab like a normal human being."

"I like mingling with the masses. Any chance of telling me why I'm here?"

"We think we got them."

"Define *think*."

"We've had a couple of little missteps or two," Nick said.

"Weren't so little," Dave said, glaring at the older man, who scowled at the young guy.

"Curtis, here," Nick said, pointing his chin at the young guy, "seems to think all white people look alike. Nailed two white guys and an Asian if you can believe it, with their girlfriends. Wasn't pretty, and wasted our time."

Curtis's expression turned morose.

"Would've helped if Biggie gave me a photo or somethin'," he said.

Biggie hauled off and slapped the back of Curtis's head, sending his hat flying like it had been launched from a cannon.

"Would've helped if God gave you the brains he gave a parrot," Biggie said.

I stared at Curtis with utter disbelief. "You shot them?"

"Nah," Biggie said. "Curtis just scraped them around the edges a touch." He threw Curtis a decidedly baleful look. "What happens when you send a boy out to do a man's work."

"Anyway," Nick continued. "On his fourth try, Curtis brought me along. Definitely Ennis."

"Where did you find him?" I said.

Curtis jumped right in.

"Put the word out to my dealers," Curtis said. "You never know, right?"

"Right."

"And sure enough, one of my homeys came through. Said this white dude and this black chick wearin' her hair in a Bob Marley do came by lookin' to score."

"Crack? Blow?"

"No. The dude interested in roids. Don't get much call for that. My boy, knowin' there's a reward out for a white guy and a black gal wearin' Rasta shit, gets suspicious and calls me. Tells the white guy to meet him in hour. He tells me. And I call Nick."

"Smart kid," I said. "Deserves a bonus."

"Deserves what I give him," Biggie said.

"So Nick gets a *cab*," Dave said, "and boogies up here."

"I'm standing up the block kind of out of the way, and sure enough Ennis shows up," Nick said. "Alone."

"Told him I'd have his shit tonight," Curtis said, looking at his watch. "'Bout an hour from now."

"And that's why you're here, Jake," Dave said.

"Got a plan?"

My brother smiled his shark grin.

"Soon as Ennis shows, we nab him," he said. "And persuade him to take us to your friend Martine."

"Kind of loose on the details, don't you think?"

"Don't worry about it," Dave said. "Everything's under control."

Not from where I sat. My brother was manic. Not in the clinical sense of the word, but in the *Dave* sense. The situation had spun out of my control, leaving only a dark chop of regret in its wake.

37

The street that served as the backdrop for the out-door bazaar where Curtis's crew did business had an eerie gloominess about it. It didn't help that the streetlights had been shot out.

Boarded-up buildings. A botanica shut down for the night. The sign for a long-gone gypsy cab service hanging at a crazy angle. A steel-shuttered fried chicken take-out joint. The corner bodega was the only retail operation that appeared to be functioning. What little light there was came from burning garbage cans over which the dealers warmed their hands.

Beacons in the night for hypes to steer their ships by.

The temperature had dipped into the low teens, and a light snow dusted everything white. Despite the weather, business was brisk. By foot and by car, dopers descended on the street like it was bargain day at Walmart. And

Curtis's crew, mostly young teenagers, was raking in the cash.

The four of us sat in the comfortable warmth of Dave's Mercedes—Nick and Curtis in front, and Dave and me in back—and waited for Ennis to appear.

"What makes you think he's coming, Curtis?" I said.

"Know my customers," he said. "Walk barefoot over broken glass to get that happy feeling."

With the resolve of a dreadnought plowing through enemy waters, a young woman, barely out of her teens, pushed a baby carriage through the gauntlet of buyers and sellers.

"She and her child shouldn't have to deal with this crap," I said.

"Ain't got no kid in there. Making a delivery. She mules for me."

Dave hooted. He was manic again, high on the prospect of the violence.

"That's my brother for you," he brayed. "Heart as big as all get-out. And never saw the sucker punch coming."

"Screw you, Dave!"

He gave me a brotherly pat on the back. "Why're you getting all serious? It was a joke. By the way, are you strapped?"

My hand strayed to the hard outline of the Glock nestled in my pocket.

"Locked and loaded," I said. "While we've got a few minutes, let's review the plan. And this time, details would be very helpful."

"Ennis shows up to make the buy," Nick said. "And Curtis here passes him the package. During the transaction, one of Curtis's guys whacks him with the bat hard enough to put him on the ground."

"More than a love tap," I said, making certain we understood each other, "but less than a swing for the fences. We need a reasonably alert Ennis, with all of his faculties more, not less, intact. Got that, Curtis?"

He flashed me a sullen nod, then turned his cap around, pulled the lid over his eyes, and settled in for the wait.

"Then," Nick continued. "I pull up. Pop the trunk. You and me throw the fucker in. And off we go to the Yellow Dog for some R & R."

"My favorite part of the evening," Dave said, wearing a manic look.

A half hour after the appointed time, Ennis still hadn't made an appearance.

Dave moved forward in his seat, his mouth next to Curtis's ear. "Where is he, Curtis?" Dave crooned.

"Fuck if I know," Curtis said.

"You said you know your customers."

Dave's fingers massaged his cheek.

Curtis couldn't see Dave giving his cheek a workout, but he heard the menace in his voice.

"I do."

Dave's voice was low and tight.

"Why do I get the feeling you don't know shit?" he said.

I put a hand on my brother's knee.

"Why don't we all relax?" I said. "Give it a bit longer."

He pushed my hand off.

"Why don't you mind your own business?"

"Dave, this is my deal, not yours."

He settled back in the seat.

"Not anymore."

"When did that happen?"

There was that shark grin again.

"Just now."

"I've got a real problem with that," I said. "You were supposed to find them and gracefully bow the hell out."

"I've got my reasons."

"I don't give a damn—"

He flashed me a deadeye look that said reason just went out the window.

"Someone looking to hurt you hurts me. Done talking about it. Don't push it, Jake."

And I didn't.

For now.

Twenty minutes passed, and still no Ennis.

Dave looked at his watch.

"Here's the deal, Curtis," he said. "You wasted my time. Not a good thing. I want this guy. If I don't get him, I'll take you. You've got three days to find the fucker. Or you're going into the barrel. One way or the other, I'm gonna have me a party. Anything you don't understand about that?"

My brother was getting real close to his personal tipping point.

Curtis opened the door and left without saying a word.

As much as I wanted Ennis, something inside of me hoped that he—and Curtis—had split to a more congenial spot in another part of the galaxy.

Freud said dreams were the royal road to the unconscious.

That insight came gratis from one of the many frustrated AA sponsors I had run through over the years. This guy happened to be a big-time psychoanalyst. And it was the only thing he said that stuck. Before he came along, I equated dream interpreters with shamans.

These days I'm not so sure.

In my dream I was back in the Bowery, and Sailor, the bum I'd met after seeing Cady's body, was front and center. Trying to tell me something. Grabbing my jacket. Pulling at me. Trying to get me to listen. But clawing my way awake was the only thing on my mind.

If Freud was right, my unconscious was giving me a wake-up call. I decided to go find out what it was trying to tell me.

The Majestic looked sadder than the last time I had been there. To the left of the entrance someone had erected a shabby little shrine commemorating Cady's demise. There was a rough wooden cross—two pieces of wood torn from a crate and nailed together—on which someone had inscribed his name with a Magic Marker. A couple of empty beer cans. And a sodden, brown teddy bear that looked like it had been plucked out of a garbage can.

A middle-aged guy with acne scars and a head shaped like it had had a bit of a misadventure as it traveled down the birth canal sat in Cady's old spot behind the metal-gated counter, reading a newspaper.

I gave him my card.

He was unimpressed.

"Whattya want?" he said.

"Looking for a guy named Sailor."

He went back to his newspaper.

I wrapped a five spot around another card and laid it on the counter.

"Why don't we try this again," I said.

The five disappeared into his shirt pocket, and my card elicited more than a flicker of interest.

"Wish I could help, but he's not registered at this establishment at this time," he said.

I was surprised he could string so many words together.

"Might you know where I can find him?"

"Sailor doesn't usually confide in me. But assuming he did, it's gonna cost you more."

My patience was at an end.

My hand shot through the bars and latched on to his throat.

"If you don't stop bullshitting me, I'm going to rip out your Adam's apple. Are you getting my drift here?"

I released my grip to allow him to respond.

"Now, where were we?" I said.

"I was just joking with you," he said, massaging his throat. "Everybody knows I'm a kidder."

"Great. You're a regular Don Rickles. Now, let's get back to Sailor."

"Don't know where he is. Ain't seen him in a long time."

"Where does he hang?"

"Anyplace where a couple bucks buys a bottle of Bird."

"Can we narrow that down?"

An old man shuffled up to me.

"You looking for Sailor?" he said.

"Yeah."

"He's gone."

"To where?"

"To dead. About a week ago. Found him in an alley all froze up."

"Sorry to hear that."

"Used to say he wanted to hobo it down to a sunny clime 'fore he got gathered up. Funny word, *clime*. Never heard it before. Guess he never made it."

I gave the old man a ten, and left the Majestic with no destination in mind. Eventually, I wound up outside a tiny church in Chinatown. My wedding was the last time I had been in any house of worship. But Sailor was dead, and here I was. Kismet? Freud? Or a combination of the two?

Didn't matter.

I went in and lit a candle for Sailor, and wished him an eternity of sunny climes.

38

That night I caught up with Dave and Anthony at Feeney's. They appeared to be getting along.

"Still haven't heard from Curtis," Dave said.

"After you laid out his options, I'm sure he's all over it."

"Better be. I wasn't kidding. Him or Ennis. Makes no difference."

"Who are these guys?" Anthony asked.

"Curtis is a skank drug dealer who gave me his word and hasn't delivered," Dave said. "And Ennis wants to douse your uncle's pilot light."

"Any reason?"

"When it comes to my family," Dave said, "doesn't have to be a reason. The want equals the deed."

"Your father's definition of true love," I said.

"You got a problem with that, Jake?" Dave said.

"You might say. If and when Curtis calls, I'm going to handle it. Alone."

"So, we're back to that again."

"You bet."

"You watch a lot of television, right, Jake?" Dave said.

"Far too much."

"And you like those nature shows."

"Your point?"

"You're the college guy in the family, so I figure if you like that stuff there's got to be something in it. So the other night I'm watching this show about killer whales. There's this mother orca with her baby. And she's teaching it how to hunt."

"Where're you going with this, Dave?"

"Just bear with me. So Mama Orca cuts this seal from the pod, knocks it around, flips it in the air a couple times, and takes the fight out of it."

I saw the tension build in Anthony's face, and got up from the table.

"Save it, Dave," I said.

"Wait," Dave said. "We're getting to the good part."

"There's no good part."

"Yeah, there is. So now, Mama Orca, teaching by example, sort of nudges junior into the fray. See, she's telling the little guy that if he doesn't learn to hunt and eat, he's gonna die. And that's why I'm coming with you." He looked directly at his son. "And so's Anthony, here. If he wants to be in this business, gotta get him off Mama's milk and give him a taste for blood."

I couldn't even begin to decipher the expression on Anthony's face.

"Nicely put," I said. "I'll be at the bar."

I sidled up to Nick.

"You hear that?" I said.

"Your brother's nuts," Nick said. "But, like they say, there's a method to his madness."

"Every time I think I've got him figured, he surprises me."

"That's what's kept him alive for so long. How do you think he survived guys like Jimmy Coonan, Spillane, Mickey Featherstone, and the other Westie Irish donkeys who were hell-bent on murdering each other? These guys were stone killers who would take your arms off with a nail file for the sheer joy of it. Anytime you were around those psychos, a bloodbath broke out."

"Hell of a legacy to hand down to his son."

Nick shrugged. "No one forced Anthony into it. He enlisted."

Nick's cell phone chirped.

"I gotta take this," he said.

He turned his back to me. All I heard was "We'll be right there."

He dropped the phone in his pocket.

"It's on."

Ennis was due at ten.

We drove up to Harlem and parked down the street from Curtis's dealers.

"Where's that fuck, Curtis?" Dave said.

"He's here," Nick said.

Fifteen minutes after the appointed hour, Ennis showed up. Nick saw him first, ambling down the street without a care in the world.

That was about to change in a hurry.

"It's showtime," Dave said, in a low voice.

Curtis seemed to appear out of nowhere, and sauntered up to Ennis. They exchanged a few words. Curtis pulled a small package out of his pocket and held it out. Ennis reached inside his pants pocket. That was as far as he got. A tall, gangly kid came up behind Ennis and cold-cocked him. Ten minutes later, we were in the storeroom of the Yellow Dog, the club up in Harlem.

Nick did the honors. He hauled Ennis's limp body into a wheeled desk chair and wrapped him to it with duct tape.

Dave kicked the chair with Ennis in it across the floor and sent it crashing into a wall. Then he turned to me.

"It's time for you to take a hike, Jake," he said.

"What're you going to do?"

"Find out where his girlfriend's holed up. But you're not gonna be around to enjoy the show."

"Dave . . ."

His eyes went cold.

"You're my brother and I love you," he said. "But it's time for you to go. Don't make me do something I don't want to do."

I looked over at Nick, but he shrugged and turned

away. The time for arguing was done. My brother's resident monster had come out to play.

"Come on, kid," Dave said to Anthony. "School's in."

Sleep was totally off the table. So were Allie and DeeDee. DeeDee was right. I wasn't letting either her or Allie in, and probably never would. Why inflict my snakes on them?

While Dave spent the night teaching Anthony how to become his father, I spent it wandering the city. At about four in the morning, I cashed in my chips and went home.

At eight, I reached out to Luce.

"You sound terrible, Jackson," she said.

"Pretty much sums things up."

"What's going on?"

"I'm real close to reporting a crime."

Her voice immediately switched to cop mode.

"Who? What? When? And where?"

"I said real close. Not quite there yet."

"But you want to talk about it."

"Hypothetically. For now."

"You want to get together?"

"Nope. Rather just talk it out now. I'm kind of doing a toe dance on the horns of a moral dilemma, and I'd like your input."

"OK."

"Let's say there was a really bad guy who wound up in a bind. His mission in life was to end yours. Instead, he wound up in the hands of a much badder guy whose mission in life was to protect you."

"What's Dave up to now?" Luce asked.

"Off the record?"

"Maybe we ought to end this conversation right now."

"I didn't get to the dilemma," I said.

"Be careful, Jackson."

"What would you do?"

"My head tells me that we don't need any more dead bodies littering the streets of this fair city. But my heart tells me that one less person trying to kill you is a good thing. Is that noncommittal enough for you?"

It wasn't noncommittal at all.

39

left my apartment, grabbed a cab, and headed back up to Harlem.

The guy with the medallion was standing in front of the Yellow Dog.

"Remember me?" I said.

He gave me the once-over.

"No," he said.

"Name's Steeg. I'm with the folks in the storeroom. Check with Biggie if you've got a problem with that."

His huge brow furrowed as he considered his next move.

"No need," he finally said. "Go on in. Biggie's in the club. He says it's OK, it's OK."

"Appreciate it."

"Man, whatever's going on in there is truly fucked up."

"You've been inside?"

"Wouldn't go in there if that was my momma screamin'. Just standin' out here and listenin' to that shit gives me the creeps."

Biggie sat at a table drinking whiskey straight.

He looked up at me, and slowly shook his head.

"Bad business," he said.

"They in the back?"

He filled a shot glass with whiskey and downed it. Then he nodded.

"What a night," he said.

I left Biggie to his thoughts and walked into the store-room.

It looked like a Jackson Pollock drip painting from hell. Ennis's blood spatter adorned the walls, the packing crates, the floor . . . and my brother, who had stripped down to his shirtsleeves.

Ennis, still taped to the chair, looked like he had fallen into a thresher.

I thought I was going to be sick.

Anthony stood off to the side wearing a dazed look. Bits of what I guessed was his own puke dotted his shirt. Tommy Cisco stood next to him, his battered face wearing an amused look.

But the big surprise was that Martine was in attendance. And unmarked. Standing right behind her was Nick, with a gun trained on her back.

"The party's over, Dave," I said.

"Nah," he said. "It's only just starting."

"It's done."

He gestured at Ennis with the stump of his hand.

"Look at the hard guy," he said. "If you took a saber saw to my eyes, I wouldn't spill my guts. This fucker didn't think twice about giving his girlfriend up."

"Steeg, please," Martine pleaded. "He said he's going to kill us. All I did was run a whorehouse. You don't die for that."

"You tried to kill my brother, bitch!" Dave said.

"I talked to Randi," I said. "You didn't run whores. You destroyed them. But even you don't deserve this."

I turned to my brother, and kept my voice as even as I could.

"School's out," I said. "I'm taking them with me, Dave. Turning them over to the cops."

"Ain't gonna happen."

"Dave."

"Nobody fucks with my brother."

"We both know this isn't about me. Never was."

He looked over at Cisco.

"It's time for you to do your thing, Tommy," Dave said.

Cisco nodded, and pulled a piece from his waistband. Ambled over. And held it to my head.

"Back away," he said.

"You're not serious, Dave," I said.

"As nuns at High Mass," Dave said.

I didn't move.

"You know this ends it between us," I said.

He smiled. "It never ends, Jake. It's you and me forever and ever. Amen."

"Nick," he said. "Give me your piece."

Nick reluctantly handed my brother his gun.

"Anthony," my brother said, holding the gun out. "First, Ennis. And then, her."

But Anthony was in another place.

"*Anthony!*"

He blinked a few times as if coming out of a deep sleep.

Then his body moved.

He took the gun, and pointed it at Ennis.

"Anthony!" I yelled.

The muzzle pressed hard against my temple.

"Don't even think about it," Cisco muttered.

"Go on, Anthony," Dave prompted. "Do him."

The gun wavered in Anthony's hand.

Seconds passed.

"Anthony," I said. "Listen to me. This isn't who you are. Just tell your father to go fuck himself. And walk away."

"You can do this, kid," Dave urged. "I know you can. Just pull the trigger. And it's done. It's easy."

Anthony's hand steadied.

And then Ennis's eyes opened and fixed on Anthony.

He lowered the gun.

"I can't," he said.

For a few moments Dave just stared at him.

"You're sure," he said.

Anthony nodded. "I can't."

Dave took the gun and patted his son on the cheek.

"You did good, kid," he said. "Go home. I'll take it from here."

Dave turned to Ennis.

"Now you get to choose who's gonna be first," he said. "You or your girlfriend."

Cisco lowered his gun and I walked up to my brother.

"Give me the gun, Dave," I said.

"Not a fucking chance. They tried to hurt you, and they're going to pay."

And then everything went to hell in a hurry. And it happened in a flash.

As I went for the gun, Martine made a break for the door.

And Anthony came alive.

His hand shot out and grabbed her dreads. The other hand wound up under her chin.

And he yanked.

She tried to pull away.

He yanked harder. Twisting and pulling.

Until there was the sound of a tree limb snapping.

Martine went limp.

Anthony didn't release his grip until her body slid to the floor.

My brother looked down at Martine. When he looked

back up, it seemed as if his world had suddenly gone dark.

He turned to Nick.

"Make the garbage disappear."

Then he turned to his son.

"Looks like graduation day after all."

40

Two weeks later, Nick showed up at my door.

"Did my brother send you?" I said.

I hadn't spoken to Dave since that morning up in Harlem. Hadn't shown up at Feeney's on the chance that I'd run into him.

"Does it matter?"

"No."

"Can I come in?"

"No beef with you."

He sat down at my kitchen table.

"Maybe you're misreading things," he said.

"I know what I saw."

"I saw it too. Could've been an accident."

"The possibility had occurred to me. But then I eighty-sixed it."

"Why's that?"

"When Anthony couldn't bring himself to kill Ennis, in his screwed-up mind he was letting his father down. But when given a second chance, he stepped up to the plate."

"I don't know about that. Maybe things just got out of hand, like."

"You really missed your calling, Nick. Would've made a fortune as a political spinmeister."

"Ain't spinning nothing. Your brother's not happy at the way things turned out. We both know he never wanted this for his kid."

"Tough shit! You break it, you bought it. And all the king's horses and all the king's men aren't going to put Anthony back together again."

"So your brother isn't the greatest parent in the world. He tried tough love, and it bit him in the ass. Does that mean you get to turn your back on him? He is what he is."

"In my world it does."

"Then you're as fucked up as he is," Nick said. "You're all he's got, Steeg. Without you around as a brake, he's headed straight for an abutment."

"And after all that went down, you expect me to give a damn?"

"Since you were kids, is there anything he wouldn't do for you? Do you know how many times he's saved your ass? How many shellackings he took from Dominic for you, and never said a word?"

"More than a few," I had to admit.

"And then there was that priest at Most Precious Blood. You were about ten. Made your life hell because you were smart and asked too many good questions that the guinea fuck couldn't answer."

"Father Riccio."

Riccio was the bane of my youth. Had this long, thick dowel. When he wasn't slamming it in the palm of his hand to underscore the moral lesson of the day, he would give me a couple of whacks and then make me kneel on it for an hour or two. Man of true faith.

"And then it stopped, didn't it?"

"I wondered about that."

"Well, you can stop wondering. Your brother kicked the living shit out him. Told him he'd kill him if he ever laid a hand on you again. And he would've."

"What do you want from me, Nick?"

"Not what I want. It's what he needs."

"And what's that?"

He got up and walked to the door.

"He'll be at Feeney's tomorrow at noon. Keep it light."

"Is Anthony still in the business?"

"Who the hell knows?"

"Last question. What happened to Ennis?"

"See you tomorrow," Nick said.

The next day, at noon, I showed up at Feeney's. Dave and Anthony were sitting in a booth in the back with Sal Lomascio.

Dave lit up when he saw me.

"Look what the cat dragged in, Sallie," he said. It took everything I had to keep it light.

"Good to see you again, Sal."

"How's it going, Steeg?" he said.

"Fair to middling," I said. I turned to my brother and his son. "You two are looking well."

"Started going to the gym," Dave said. "Me and Anthony. Teaching him how to box. Maybe one day he'll take me."

Anthony smiled. "The way it's going, I'll be punch drunk long before that day ever comes."

All this bonding stuff was giving me a dizzy spell. But I went with it.

"Your uncle Jake could show you a thing or two," Dave said. "Golden Gloves champ. Middleweight."

"I fought in the Gloves," Sal said with a twitch of his mustache. "Never made it past the prelims. I'm impressed, Steeg."

"Don't be. The guy I was supposed to fight in the finals got busted and didn't show up."

"Come on," Dave said. "You're selling yourself short. You could've made it as a pro."

"Right. I could've been a contender. Come on! Fighting three-rounders and winding up as a tomato can was more like it."

Anthony got up.

"Be right back," he said. "Going to the john."

I waited until he was out of earshot.

"How's he doing?"

"Anthony? Thanks to me, not so hot."

"Contrition fits you well, Dave."

He flashed me a lopsided grin.

"Working on it, Jake," he said. "Are we square?"

"No. Not even close."

He put his hand over mine.

"But we're talking," he said. "It's a start."

Nick wandered over.

"Everything OK here?" he said.

"Hunky-dory," Dave said.

"That's what I like to hear. There're two broads over at the bar asking about you, Steeg."

I looked up.

Wanda and Tiffany were in the house.

"Tell them to come over," I said.

Nick walked over to them.

"You sure do hang with some interesting people, Jake," Dave said.

"Wanda hooked for Martine. It was her sister who died in the fire at your warehouse. Now it's her turn."

"What do you mean?"

"Terminal cancer."

"Life's a lottery. Winners and losers."

"Which one are we, Dave?"

"Too soon to tell. Still playing the game."

Wanda looked weaker and more pallid than the last time I had seen her. Just walking to our table was an effort.

I made the introductions.

"You don't have to worry about Martine and Ennis anymore, Wanda," I said.

"What do you mean?"

I glanced at Dave. "They're not gonna bother you anymore."

"See, honey," Tiffany said. "I told you Steeg would take care of it."

"What happened?" Wanda said.

"All you need to know is they're out of the picture," Dave said.

"People like them always come back," Wanda said.

Dave smirked. "Only if they're Christ."

"Join us for lunch?" I asked.

"Appreciate the offer," Tiffany said. "But we're on our way. Just dropped by to thank you, and say good-bye."

"So it's off to Rochester," I said. "And the house with the white picket fence. I'm really happy for you."

"Rochester's gonna have to wait a few days. Wanda wants to make a stop in a little town outside Des Moines first."

"I really would rethink that if I were you, Wanda," I said.

"No," she said. "I think Daddy needs to see what's become of his little girl. Mommy, too."

I thought of what Luce said about decisions that came from the head or the heart. I could give the Klempers a heads-up that Wanda was on the way. But my heart said no. The statute of limitations ran out a long time ago for Jonas and Adele. And since I didn't put much stock in eternal damnation, this was the only way they'd get what was coming to them. Could she pull it off? Given the shape she was in, I was betting against. But if her want kept her going a little while longer, who was I to argue?

I got up and threw my arms around her.

"You take care now," I said.

"I—"

Her body stiffened. Then sagged against mine.

"What's wrong?"

"My God!" she whispered. "It's him. The man I saw outside the warehouse. The one who looked like Death."

I turned and saw Anthony walking toward us.

41

To avoid a scene, I hustled Wanda and Tiffany out of Feeney's with assurances that I would handle things.

It turned out to be an empty promise.

"What was that all about?" Anthony said.

"Just some friends. One of them is real sick. Put them in a cab and sent them home."

"From the look of her it's a wonder she can stay upright," Dave said.

"Anthony," I said. "Would you excuse us? I'd like to talk to your father alone."

"You want me to go too?" Sal said.

"No," Dave said. "Stay."

"No problem," Anthony said. "I'll check in with you later, Pop."

I waited until Anthony was out the door.

"What's going on, Jake?" Dave said.

"There's a problem."

"I'm not up for this."

"I know who burned down your warehouse. Wanda just told me."

"And that would be?"

"Your son."

"Get the fuck outta here!"

Expecting a reaction, I looked over at Sal but his face betrayed nothing.

"It's true," I said.

"Because some two-buck whore said so?"

"Because she was there, and saw him."

He ran his hand through his hair.

"She saw him?" he repeated.

"Clear view of his face. Scared the hell out her. Said she'd never forget what he looked like."

"So if Anthony hadn't gone to the john, and the two hookers didn't just happen to stop by, Anthony would have skated. Hell of a coincidence."

"Or maybe magical forces in the universe interested in balancing the scales."

He leaned back and the color drained from his face.

"I get indicted," Dave said. "And almost wind up in the slam for the rest of my life. You go looking for the torch. And it turns out he lives in my own house. Can you beat it?"

"The question is, what are you going to do about it?"

"What do you expect me to do?"

"The fire took a lot of people, Dave."

"So, what's it to me? Who gives a shit about a couple or three dead street people?"

"You sound like the roaches are crawling over your brainpan again."

He considered that for a few seconds.

"Fucking kid," he said. "What was in his head?"

"Want me to play armchair psychiatrist?"

"Your nickel. Give it a go."

"His way of making you pay for fucking up his family, and his life. You drove his mother away. He loves you and tries to be like you, and all you do is ridicule him. Tell him he's a moron. What the hell do you expect?"

"So we're back to the sins of the father."

"Looks that way. But let's get back to my question. How're you going to square this thing?"

"That's easy. Give them the torch."

42

"We got us a problem, Jackson," Luce said.

For the first time all winter my apartment was toasty warm. I was settling in to an evening of Willie Nelson CDs when she called.

"This hasn't been a great day, Luce."

"Well, it's about to get worse."

"How worse?"

"DeeDee's boyfriend Justin was busted. I'll meet you at Midtown North."

Luce met me in the lobby.

"What happened?" I said.

"He beat up a kid."

"No way. He reads *Scientific American* to let steam off."

"Not today. Got into it with some other kid at a basketball court. Someone called the cops. Got him on an assault."

"What were they fighting about?"

"Wouldn't say. Neither would the other kid. But Justin was doing most of the punching when the cops got there. So he won the lottery and got to wear the bracelets."

"What's the other kid's name?"

"Matt Gershon. Attends Devereaux Academy."

"So does Justin."

"What's the world coming to?" Luce said. "Probably arguing over osmosis or something."

"Is he all right?"

"Far as I can see."

"Where is he?"

"In a holding cell."

When a kid like Justin gets penned in with men who have been through the system several times, he immediately becomes a target.

"Anybody else in there with him?"

"Give me some credit, Jackson," Luce said. "Had to combine a couple of cells, but he's got an empty one. For now."

"Does his father know?"

"Doubt it. He refused his courtesy phone call."

"I assume DeeDee doesn't know either," I said. "She'd be here if she did. Can I see him?"

The first thing that hits you in the holding cell area is the smell. A combination of unwashed bodies, puke, and some other malodorous stuff I couldn't even begin to put a name to. The second thing that hits you is the bleakness.

Justin stood in the corner with his head hanging down. As I approached, he lifted his head and walked up to the bars.

"How're you doing, Justin?" Luce said.

"OK."

"Want to call your dad?"

He shook his head.

"Fine. I'll leave you two to talk. Jackson, you know where to find me."

"What's this all about, kiddo?" I said.

He refused to make eye contact.

"Nothing."

"You keep that attitude up and you're going to take a ride through the system. I'm talking the back of a police van downtown to the holding pens, arraignment, followed by a world of woe. You're going to be with people you truly don't want to spend a minute with. You up for that, son?"

"We were fooling around," he said. "And things just got out of hand."

"Things getting out of hand usually means pushing and shouting. Not beating the living shit out of someone."

"Can I just go home?"

"Only shot is by leveling with me, Justin. Then maybe I can make this go away."

His chin dropped to his chest.

"Nothing to talk about," he said. "We were shooting

hoops, and things just got out of control. I didn't mean to hit him. It just kind of happened."

"And that's all you're gonna tell me."

"Nothing more to say. Look, my father needs me. I can't stay here. He's expecting me home."

"OK, Justin. I'll see what I can do. Anything I can get you?"

"Yeah. Out of here."

Luce was waiting for me at her desk.

"What did he have to say?" she said.

"About what you'd expect. Just horsing around, and things sort of spun out of control."

"You believe him?"

"No reason not to. At least until I talk to the vic."

"Isn't the first time for Justin," Luce said.

"What do you mean?"

"From what I've been able to find out, he's had some other brushes with the police."

"You're not serious."

"Fighting mostly. Shrinks call it acting out. And the cops have always cut him a break and turned him loose with warnings. The fact that he goes to Devereaux Academy carries some weight."

"The kid has plenty to act out about," I said. "Mother's dead. Father's paralyzed from the waist down. I met him. Depends on Justin for pretty much everything."

"Doesn't excuse him, Jackson. Hard lives is something this city does real well."

"I know."

"But you're going to ask for a favor anyway."

"I am. Any chance you can give Justin a desk appearance ticket and cut him loose? I promise I'll get to the bottom of this. The kid doesn't belong here."

"Under normal circumstances, no. But for you, Jackson . . ."

"Appreciate it."

"No problem," she said. "But DeeDee sure has a lot to learn about men."

"That she does," I said.

"I'll get the paperwork going. Justin should be out of here in an hour or so."

"One other thing."

She gave an exasperated sigh.

"You're using up all your chits, Jackson. What now?"

"DeeDee is as close to a daughter as I'll probably ever have. And Justin's acting out bothers me. I just wonder if there's anything else that I don't know."

"And you want me to run him through our computers."

"Wouldn't hurt," I said.

Justin was released forty-five minutes later. I put him in a cab and sent him home. He asked me not to tell DeeDee what had happened. It was a promise I couldn't make. I needed her to point out the kid he'd sparred with, Matt Gershon.

That evening I took DeeDee out to dinner and broke the news.

"I don't believe it, Steeg," she said. "Not Justin. He's the kindest, most gentle person I've ever known." She pulled out her cell phone. "I've got to call him."

"Not a good idea. He's been through a lot, and has a lot more to think about."

"But I care about him. And I want him to know."

"Believe me, kiddo, he knows. But there is something you can do for me that would help Justin."

"Anything. Just name it."

"I want to talk to Matt Gershon. Can you point him out to me?"

"Matt? That's who Justin was fighting with? And they were playing basketball in this weather?"

"Seems so."

"How dumb is that?"

"Way dumb."

"Matt's a jerk. No one likes him."

"And I'm sure with good reason. But I still need to talk to him."

"He's in my English class. First period tomorrow."

"I'll be there," I said.

The next morning DeeDee and I hopped a cab down to Devereaux Academy. We got to the school fifteen minutes before first period and waited out front.

Five minutes later Matt Gershon showed up.

"That's him," DeeDee said.

Turns out I didn't need DeeDee. Matt, a thin, little guy with really long hair, sported a major-league black eye, and a sizable bruise up near his right cheekbone.

I stopped him at the door.

"Matt?" I said, flashing my card. "My name is Steeg. I need to talk to you about Justin Hapner."

He seemed annoyed.

"I told you people everything I know," he said.

"Which was nothing. Justin may go to jail. Do you want that on your conscience?"

He put his hand to face. "Do you see what he did to me?"

"Doesn't look like it was fun."

"Anything but," Matt said. "But I don't want to talk about it. It's over and done with."

"Not quite. I just have one question."

"I'm late for a test."

He tried to brush past me.

Fat chance.

"Matt, my friend," I said. "You're going to be subpoenaed as a witness. That means testifying at Justin's trial. And his defense attorney will pull out all the stops to impeach you and your testimony. That means going through your life with a fine-tooth comb looking for anything that casts a shadow on your credibility. You wouldn't believe the stuff they can find. Maybe your weed stash. Maybe something else. It's the way things work in the real world. Do you really want that?"

"I have rights too." The words were right, but the self-assurance was beginning to crack.

"Sure you do. You're a smart kid who seems to know how things work. And you know you can make life really easy if you just answer one question."

He looked at his watch.

"I'm late for class."

"Just one question, Matt."

He checked his watch again.

"Fine," he said.

"What provoked Justin into throwing a punch?"

"The whole thing was stupid. He drove for a layup and missed."

"And?"

"I said it was a faggy shot."

43

was tired of dancing at the Sinners' Ball. Anthony takes down Dave's warehouse because he can't take his father down. Angela dead, and Wanda right behind her because the Klempers put them there. Justin goes off on a classmate and winds up in jail because he can't maintain an erection. And the murderer of at least nine men still on the loose. It put me in mind of spending the rest of my life in a closet.

And then my cell phone chirped. I had dumped the George Jones ring days earlier. Too depressing.

It was Luce.

"What's up?" I said.

"You asked me to check on Justin. Remember?"

"For the sake of my sanity, please tell me you found nothing."

"All right. I found nothing."

"Really?"

"Oh yeah. Absolutely nothing."

"Why don't you sound happy about it?"

"Jackson, you're not following me here. There are no records. No birth certificate. Nothing."

"How can that be?"

"I don't know. He either arose spontaneously or his records fell through the bureaucratic cracks somewhere along the way, or someone's lying. Damndest thing I ever saw."

I tried calling Justin several times, but no one answered.

To jump-start my happy place, I had dinner with Allie at a quaint little French/Vietnamese restaurant in the village. But this time I was the one picking at the food.

"You look like you need a friend, Steeg," she said.

I reached over and took her hand.

"You're my friend," I said.

"Don't ever doubt it."

"Then cheer me with stories of the advertising whirl. Fill my heart with laughter, and snap me out of this damned blue funk I'm hopelessly mired in."

"The last few months have been bad, haven't they?"

"That's putting too fine a point on it. "

"Want to talk about it?"

"Wouldn't it be a wonderful world if kids could pick their parents? Something like an online dating service where couples are forced to post their life résumés, warts and all, and kids get to interview them and try them out before they commit."

"Are we talking about your brother and his son?"

"And my father. And tons of other screwed-up people walking the streets who have kids and then actively destroy their lives."

I didn't want to weigh her down with the tragic tale of Wanda and Angela.

"I find that difficult to relate to," Allie said.

"So you had a happy childhood?"

"Ecstatic."

"And you had Herbie Aronson."

"Old Herbie. You remembered!"

"How could I forget your first love serenading you on the piano on warm summer nights."

"Yes, but his repertoire was limited to one song. 'Big Rock Candy Mountain.' That's all he knew, but he played it gloriously."

That triggered my memory of what Sailor had said.

"It's funny you mention that. I ran into a panhandler down in the Bowery. He didn't say much except that he hoped to see the deceased, a guy named Walter Cady, at the Big Rock Candy Mountain one day. Had no idea what he was talking about. As I remember, it's a kid's folk song."

"It is now. But it didn't start out that way."

"What do you mean?"

"Since Herbie played it so well, I wanted to learn the lyrics so I could sing along. I had this vision of Herbie playing it at concerts. And me, in my evening gown, leaning against the piano, belting it out."

"All this at ten?"

"Told you I was precocious. So I went to the Brooklyn Public Library and found the lyrics. And guess what?"

"What?"

"There are two sets. The original, and the sanitized version which eventually was recorded. Most people think the song is a merry little ditty about a place where your birthday's every week and it's Christmas every day. But it's not."

"Could have fooled me."

"It's a ballad about a child being lured with magical stories of the Big Rock Candy Mountain, and ultimately being kidnapped into a hobo camp. Want to hear an original verse?"

"After all these years you remember?"

"Impossible to forget. It was my first hint that the world could be an awful place. When you hear it, you'll see why. Here goes.

The punk rolled up his big blue eyes
And said to the jocker, "Sandy,
I've hiked and hiked and wandered too,
But I ain't seen any candy.
I've hiked and hiked till my feet are sore
And I'll be damned if I hike any more
To be buggered sore like a hobo's whore
In the Big Rock Candy Mountains."

"'To be buggered sore like a hobo's whore'?" I said.

"Not pretty, is it?"

Suddenly everything fit.

Troy Hapner's shiner. No infant photos of Justin. No photos of his mother. His inability to perform with DeeDee. The fag comment from Matt Gershon. The shrinking intervals between the killings. The connection to Dave's warehouse. Spinning out of control. Working his way back to . . .

I bolted from the table.

"Allie," I said. "Find DeeDee and stay with her until you hear from me."

All the lights in the Hapner's apartment were out and the door was locked.

I kicked it in, switched on the lights, and moved quickly past the kitchen into the living room.

Troy Hapner was lying on the floor in a widening pool of blood. His eyes were closed. But he was breathing.

I knelt down and smacked him awake.

"Where's Justin, you son of a bitch?"

His eyes blinked open and tried to focus.

"Help . . . me! Please."

I grabbed a handful of his hair and yanked his head up.

"Where's Justin, you sick bastard?"

His hand strayed to his bloody crotch. "Don't . . . know. Look . . . did . . . this . . . to me."

I got to my feet and went looking for Justin.

I didn't have far to go.

He was hanging from a chinning bar he had set up in the doorway of the closet in his room.

Another ghost to haunt my nights.

His body was cold.

I checked for a pulse.

An ineffable sadness swept over me.

I walked past Troy Hapner and into the kitchen. Snatched a bread knife from the counter, went back to the bedroom, and cut Justin down. After gathering him in my arms, I laid him on his bed, and covered him with a blanket.

Then I sat down next to him.

It was a deathwatch. A mourning for a kid who never had a chance.

A long time passed before I finally got up to leave.

In the living room, Troy Hapner lay where I had left him.

His eyes followed me as I moved toward the door.

"Please," he begged. "Help . . . me!"

I closed the door behind me.

44

A week later, Luce called. Wanted me to meet her at the precinct house. Said she had some information for me.

We met in an interrogation room on the second floor. A pile of file folders sat in the middle of the table.

"How're you holding up, Jackson?"

"Better than DeeDee. Hooked her up with a therapist."

"How's that going?"

"She said it's going to take a while, but DeeDee should come out the other end reasonably OK."

"Do you believe her?"

"Time'll tell," I said. "But I had a sit-down with her father."

"How'd that go?"

"Kept it pretty basic. Told him DeeDee needs a father,

not a habitual recidivist. Told him I'd throw him off a roof if he ever strayed off the reservation again."

"Did he promise to behave?"

"Absolutely."

"Do you believe him?"

"Absolutely not. Fucking cretin! I've also been to the Dominican embassy trying to get a line on her mother."

"Any luck?"

"Not yet."

"Anything I can do?"

"What you have been doing. Be her friend. Any word on the departmental trial?"

"Went *poof*!"

"What a surprise."

"Martine and Ennis's deaths barely made the newspapers. And the word's come down that we shouldn't be investigating their homicide too hard. So the lid is still on. Tight. The rich clients breathe a sigh of relief and find a new escort service. Everyone gets to walk away. Including me."

"The way of the world. So, what have you got for me?"

Luce pointed to the pile of file folders.

"This represents all we know about Justin. You're welcome to go through them. Take all the time you need. But I figured I'd give you the short version."

"OK."

"We took a sample of Justin's DNA and sent it to the FBI, Interpol, and anywhere else they maintain a database.

We got a hit in Canada. Toronto. They maintain a DNA database of missing children."

"God bless 'em."

"Justin's real name is Dylan Salamore. He was snatched from a playground when he was three. Mother turned her back for a minute, and he was gone."

I was clenching my fists so hard, my nails dug into the palms of my hand.

"Go on," I said.

"From what we've been able to piece together from Hapner's computer—Troy Hapner is his real name—he took him to the States and began pimping him. Started with selling photos and videos of Justin—Dylan—on the Web and moved on to setting him up with a string of pedophiles all over the country."

"A childhood any kid would want."

"This went on for years, and then Justin began to age out. At roughly the same time, Hapner wrecked his car while delivering Dylan to some freak."

"Justin said that his mother was killed in the accident. But I never saw any photos of her at the apartment, because there was no mom."

"And Justin probably believed his mom was dead. He was young enough when Hapner took him that he could've brainwashed the kid into believing the story. Anyway, the accident left Hapner paralyzed from the waist down. Suddenly Hapner needed Justin. So he kept him around to do the heavy lifting."

"But what he didn't count on," I said, "was the kid becoming something of a genius, and getting into Troy's computer."

"Bingo. Justin apparently tracked down the men who used him. We have the list. And I'm not giving it to you. Some of them are dead. Some left the country. And some are in prison. Justin did what he could with what he had."

"And Nick showed him and DeeDee the warehouse, maybe even told them it wasn't getting much use. The perfect dumping ground."

"It fit his needs, and he went with it. And that's about it."

"And he was working his way back to Hapner."

"One sicko at a time. And saving the worst for last."

"What now?"

"We contacted his parents. His body was shipped to them today."

"Wish you would have told me."

"You said your good-byes, Jackson."

Her eyes began to well up.

"He deserved a lot better than he got," she said.

"Don't they all."

45

"What happens now, Dave?"

"You'll see," he said.

Dave had invited me over to his house for a take-out dinner. Said there was something special he wanted to show me. After we ate, he led me outside.

It was just before midnight and we were on the patio. Except for the feeble light of a few stars, the sky was charcoal black. The wind blowing off the river drove the temperature down to near zero. But Dave was as excited as a kid on Christmas morning.

With a star map in one hand, he fiddled with the knobs of his new telescope with the other.

"This fucker set me back a couple of thousand dollars and I ain't seen anything worth a shit yet," he said.

As usual we were talking crosswise. I wanted to

talk about Anthony, and he had the solar system on his mind.

"It's the ambient light from the city," I said. "Makes it hard to peer into the cosmos."

After some more fiddling and a couple of peeks through the eyepiece, he threw up his hands. "Fuck it! Let's go inside. I'm freezing."

Once in the house, he headed for the bar and poured himself a glass of white wine.

"I'm off the hard stuff," he said, noting the surprised look on my face. "Decided to get back in shape. Working out every day."

"Any specific reason?"

"Sound body, sound mind," he said. "Went through a bad spell. Not gonna happen again."

"Can't wait to meet the new you."

He raised a suspicious eyebrow. "I tell you I'm a new man and you think I'm full of shit."

"And your son? Is he a new man?"

He took a sip of the wine. "Leave him out of this."

"Hard to do, Dave."

He set the glass down, walked over to the window, and looked up at the sky. I walked up next to him.

His attention was focused on a plane banking right on its final approach to LaGuardia.

"Newark's closer, but I always hop a plane bound for LaGuardia when I'm coming back from Florida," he said. "And always sit on the right side."

"Why's that?"

"The city. Looks like paradise."

"Let's get back to your son. You said you were going to give the police the torch."

"I did."

"You gave Anthony up?"

"Get serious. Tommy Cisco is gonna take the fall. Worked a plea deal. Ten years, and out in five with good behavior."

"*What*?"

"Remember when he flicked the cigarette at the homeless guy? Fucking Cisco has no heart, and it's gonna cost him. Besides, I never liked the little prick anyway."

"Tell me you're kidding."

"You know me well enough to know I don't joke about family. Cisco confessed, and Sal was the witness."

"How did you get Cisco to agree to this?"

"Laid out his options."

"And Sal?"

He smiled. "We go way back."

"So much for scruples."

He turned to me.

"What do you want from me, Jake?"

"Anthony."

"He's his own man."

"Not while you're around."

He stared at me for a few seconds and then turned and looked back out the window.

"Y'know, I got the telescope so I could see a comet."

"They're kind of rare," I said.

"What I hear. But there's one coming our way. Lulin, it's called. And the guy who sold me the telescope said I should be able to see it now. Fucked if I can find it."

"Consider yourself lucky," I said.

"Why's that?"

There's an old legend that comets are harbingers of bad tidings. But I found that I didn't have it in me to mention it.

"Give you something to look forward to."

ACKNOWLEDGMENTS

I want to thank Sal Loscuito—a good friend, and one of New York's Bravest—for helping me understand the truly horrific anatomy of a fire.

And once again, I am grateful to Julian Pavia and David Larabell for making this a better book than the one they first read.

ABOUT THE AUTHOR

IRA BERKOWITZ, a native New Yorker, is the author of the Jackson Steeg mysteries, *Old Flame* and *Family Matters,* and a two-time winner of the Washington Irving Literary Award.

Find Ira online at iraberkowitz.com

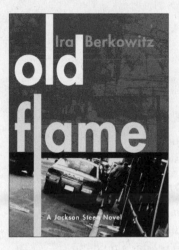